Explorer's
End

Explorer's End

H.W. Portland

Illustrated by Raven Osse

HW PORTLAND BOOKS
Orcutt, California

HW Portland Books, LLC
© 2022 by HW Portland Books

Contact information: hwportland.com
Email: hw@hwportland.com

V.B.

Published 2022

Library of Congress Control Number: 2022939501
ISBN: 979-8-9859374-0-4 (paperback)
ISBN: 979-8-9859374-1-1 (ebook)

Category: Fiction, Science Fiction, Adventure

Interior Illustrations: Raven Osse
Cover Illustration: Elias Stern

Brüder, über'm Sternenzelt Brothers, above the starry canopy
Muß ein lieber Vater wohnen. There must dwell a loving Father.
Ihr stürzt nieder, Millionen? Are you collapsing, millions?
Ahnest du den Schöpfer, Welt? Do you sense the creator, world?
Such' ihn über'm Sternenzelt! Seek him above the starry canopy!
Über Sternen muß er wohnen. Above stars must He dwell.

Friedrich Schiller, *Ode to Joy*

Chapter 1
Alan

The blood-red clouds of Eleva made the industrial purpose of the planet no secret. Thousands of years collecting the galaxy's waste and reprocessing it back into raw elements had left Eleva a polluted orb circling an aging star.

From space, the planet's thick, acrid clouds obscured the surface. The true destruction of the world revealed itself as Dr. Alan's small ship pierced through the high layers of acid haze and oily smoke.

"Etsel," Alan said, "you still got me?"

"I hear you," a man replied through the earpiece. "Welcome to the galaxy's dump."

From horizon to horizon, the surface was covered by a patchwork of sprawling cities of dark, soot-stained factories, and vast plains of refuse waiting to be processed. Yellow lights sparkled across the dreadful landscape, the only sign that the wasteland was still in use and not a relic of some long-gone civilization.

"Yeah. Charming place, this planet," Alan said.

He commanded the flight computer to land at a hangar tucked between two sprawling factories, each venting roiling black smoke into the air. He found himself in disgusted awe as the ship approached and the full scale of the buildings was revealed.

The vessel descended into the canyons of the city, its thruster stirring up the gray ash that covered the buildings like snow.

The craft settled onto its struts. Alan shut it down and peeled himself out of the pilot's seat. It was a compact shuttle, meant to ferry people between a deep-space exploration ship and planet surfaces. It lacked the comfort of a long-haul vessel, and Alan had to hunch over while moving about the tiny cabin.

"You know the ship has two seats. You could have come."

"One visit to Eleva is enough for me. I'll watch you from up here."

"OK, but next time we do something like this, let's try to arrange it someplace nice."

"Like Nadziboro?"

Alan could hear the smile in Etsel's voice.

"You'll never let me forget Nadziboro, will you?"

"Not as long as it's a great story."

"You only like that story because I was the one being chased."

He opened a closet in the aft of the ship and pulled out his respirator and a jacket. The planet's atmosphere was so saturated with fumes that respirators had to be worn even in most of the climate-controlled areas of the city. He opened the vessel door to reveal a narrow corridor littered with loose trash.

"You have our guy up?" Alan asked as he put on his respirator.

"Yeah, he got on the link while you were headed down. Name is Ebo. He's ready, and not too far from where you landed. He's at a restaurant called Rahka-Rahka. You can try a local dish."

"I think I'll pass."

"You might never get the chance to taste the fare of Eleva again."

"I can live with that."

The hallway opened to a massive atrium rippling with the activity and noise of hundreds of people milling between mazes of food stalls and vendor tables. Along the perimeter of the mall, under colorful electronic signs competing for attention, were the stores and restaurants of the bazaar. Overhead, the red clouds of Eleva were visible through a tremendous skylight.

Alan found the sign he was looking for perched above a discreet doorway. He weaved through the crowds and stopped at the steps leading to the restaurant.

"Alright. This is it. I'm going in."

"Hey," Etsel said, "be careful. This guy, Ebo, is a strange one. I don't trust him."

"I'll keep it short."

Rahka-Rahka was dark, busy, and noisy. Sixty people crammed into a room built to hold thirty. People of all forms and species stood drinking and talking in clusters against the walls and packed around small tables.

Over loud music and bar chatter, a voice rose above all others: "Alan!"

From a table at the center of the small establishment, a figure waved and caught Alan's attention. Alan pulled down his respirator and moved through the crowd. At the table was a single open chair opposite a seated man with two glowing drinks. He was slender and unkempt, his coveralls dabbled with aged stains and his oily hair matted across his brow.

"Ebo," Alan said as he settled into the chair.

"A man travels across the galaxy and joins another for a drink," said Ebo. "One man has a pocket full of money and the other has a pocket full of history. But sitting a few tables behind them are three Brabillia who have, well," Ebo pushed a drink to Alan, "a lot of muscle."

Alan looked at the drink and realized the source of the light in the cup was a small fish. The glowing creature slowly turned in the glass, lazily chasing its own tail.

"The Brabillia want the history," Ebo struggled for a word, "the artifact. But they know the man who holds it is part of a big, protective family. So they know they can't just take it from him. They can't take the artifact—until I give it to you. Do you see?"

"So, to be clear, I'm the one with the money in this story?"

Ebo frowned. He reached under the table, produced a finger-length silver cylinder, and placed it on the table. He removed its cap to produce from within a small rectangle, an inch long, metallic and etched with red and blue stripes.

Alan recognized it.

"So much money for something so small," Ebo mused.

"You don't seem like the type who would appreciate relics from the first civilization in the galaxy."

"You're right. I don't care about myths," he said as he put the artifact back in its cylinder and sealed it. "I care about the money you'll pay for it."

Alan rapped his fingers on the table in thought, then reached into his jacket and produced a metal card. He placed it on the table next to the cylinder. The man looked at the card, picked up his drink, and swallowed its contents. Alan felt a pang of regret for the fish.

Ebo hesitated for a moment, then leaned in. "Listen, traveler," he put a finger on the cylinder, "when you touch this, it is no longer mine, and they will come for it." Though he spoke to Alan, his gaze shifted to a table behind them.

Alan glanced over his shoulder. Even in the dim light of the restaurant, he could spot the group of Brabillia sitting a few tables back. The race was well known for its size, strength, and asymmetrical face. Three eyes on the right side of a stocky head with no neck, one eye on the left, all mounted on a body that had to walk sideways through doors. In a straight fight, a human faced steep odds, but if speed and agility were brought into the equation…

"Right."

Alan reached for his glass and brought the liquid to his lips, but stopped short of drinking it. He put the glowing drink back on the table and stood up from his chair.

"I'd like to stay and talk about your business ethics, but I think I have to run," Alan said.

"I should think so."

Alan held his hand over the cylinder for a moment, then snatched the object and headed for the door. Behind him, three hulking figures stood and followed, their mass jostling the crowds of seated patrons as they passed.

Ebo held up Alan's glowing drink. "You don't want the fish?"

Outside the restaurant, in the atrium, Alan tasted the noxious fumes ever present in the air and moved his respirator back over his face.

"Etsel, it's another damn Nadziboro."

"You got the artifact?"

"Yeah. And three Brabillia are tailing me. Your guy set us — me — up."

"But you got the artifact!"

"I *hate* chases!"

As he cut through the crowded mall, he caught sight of two beastly figures in front of the hangar and abruptly pivoted his stride ninety degrees.

"There are another two blocking me from the hangar. They are either smart or I have bad luck."

"Bad luck. Get on a train. At the next stop, you can summon the ship to a nearby hangar."

"Good plan, I just have to —"

Alan sensed a commotion and spun around to find the three Brabillia from Rahka-Rahka breaking through the crowd. The closest swung its fist at Alan's head. Alan fell onto his back, reflexively and without grace, the fist sailing over him. Figures in the crowd shouted in alarm and withdrew to clear space as the melee unfolded.

Alan quickly rolled and sprang to his feet. He dashed to his left and tucked his way into the throng of stunned spectators.

"Alan?" Etsel asked through the earpiece. "Are you getting to the train?"

"Working on it!"

Across the mall and past the vendors, a train platform flashed a departure notice. Behind him, three lumbering beasts parted the crowd. Alan sprinted through the shoppers, and when he reached the thick masses of commuters, he elbowed his way forward, earning the disapproval of those he cut in front of. He reached the train and slid into a crowded car, turning to see whether his pursuers had caught up. The doors sealed with no sign of the Brabillia.

After a moment, the train lurched, beginning its steady trek to the next stop. He released his breath. The cars were packed shoulder to shoulder with masked passengers; wherever he was going, many others were headed there as well.

"I got on," he said to Etsel, "but I didn't see whether my buddies did too."

"The next stop is a few minutes away. It should have a hangar, so just stay low and maybe you can get through this without a fight."

Now I know why he didn't come.

From the middle car, he began working his way through the mass of packed passengers toward the head of the train.

Out the windows, the claustrophobia of the city fell away, replaced by an endless plain of shredded industrial waste that disappeared into the horizon of red murk. The train glided twenty feet above the landscape of refuse, continuing toward a factory, passing over robotic tractors and workers moving and sorting the piles.

As he reached the lead of the train, the crowds thinned, and he found a pocket of space. From the front, he could see a conveyor belt loaded with waste tracking parallel to the rails. Its destination was the same as the train's.

Alan glanced around the car. He turned to face the window, retrieved the cylinder from his jacket, and opened it. With a gentle shake, he urged out the contents into his palm: the small rectangular artifact.

The curiosity was millions of years old, a fragment of technology from a civilization that, Alan and others suspected, had seeded the galaxy with intelligent life. Piece by piece, they were putting together a puzzle that would explain where the ancient Seed civilization had vanished to.

The sound of a scuffle caught Alan's ear, and the passengers in the car parted, revealing three Brabillia pushing their way toward him.

He closed the cylinder and put it back into his jacket.

"They found me."

"You're so close! You can't lose the artifact. Stall them, then get off the train!"

He held his hands up. "How about we get off at the next stop and work this out?"

The center Brabillia stepped forward and reached for Alan's neck. He sidestepped it, then landed a quick jab at the alien's right cluster of eyes. The creature hadn't expected a fight and stumbled back.

That trick will only work once.

The passengers moved away from the fight.

"Can you hear me?" Etsel said, anxiety welling in his voice.

"Not now!"

Alan backpedaled to the wall as the figures moved toward him. Trapped, he braced himself and yanked the red handle above his shoulder. The train's wheels locked, jolting the train and sending the Brabillia and all the standing passengers sliding forward.

Alan scrambled over the writhing pile of people that blanketed the floor and moved down the car to the second door.

"Alan, get out of there!"

"Shut up until I'm off this train!"

He realized as he shouted to the voice in his ear that he had been locking eyes with a screaming woman. Stunned, the woman quieted down.

Alan gestured to his ear. "Sorry."

"It's alright," Etsel said.

"Not you."

The train came to a stop as he wrenched the doors in the middle of the car open. As they relented, hot, acrid air poured in, and the loud clamoring of the parallel conveyor belt ten feet below the elevated rail line filled the car with noise.

Alan glanced to the front of the train where the Brabillia were emerging from the pile of passengers. He looked out at the conveyor passing below, gauged his jump, then leapt.

With a crunch and a cloud of rust, he landed on the belt and fell to his side. Hard shapes punched into his ribs and legs, eliciting a groan. He stumbled to his feet. A Brabillia jumped from the car and landed on the conveyor, falling as Alan had. The first was followed by the other two.

Alan sprinted toward them and threw all his weight into a flying kick that knocked the first Brabillia to rise off-balance and over the side of the belt. Alan worked his way to his feet and saw the other two brutes up and on their way to him. With no advantage, he ran toward the factory, leaping over piles of debris and opening some distance between him and his pursuers.

Ahead, the conveyor belt passed through a narrow arch. Alan stopped his sprint and turned to face the Brabillia, who were catching up. Reaching down to the trash under his feet, he pulled a long rod from the pile and hung its ends over the edge. As the belt passed through the arch, the rod caught the legs of the arch and leapt out of his hands.

One pursuer realized Alan's plan in time to duck under the rod. The other was caught square in the chest and dragged down the conveyor, away from the fight.

Alone, and with anger in its four eyes, the last Brabillia charged as Alan fled. The two ran down the belt, leaping and stepping over trash.

"Alan?" Etsel said through the earpiece.

"Can't. Talk." Alan struggled. "Running."

The air within the respirator had become thick and wet, his need for oxygen outweighing the respirator's ability to supply it.

A shadow fell over the belt as it entered the enormous processing plant. The interior was cavernous, hundreds of feet tall, with conveyors moving materials between massive machines and sorting lines. At the far end of the long building, smelting chambers spewed heat, smoke, and a fiery orange glow.

Twenty feet below the belts, the floor of the facility was a highway of moving tractors and transports—hundreds of labor-bots tending to equipment and unloading materials. Piles of stacked fuels, agent barrels, and manipulators dotted the floor, the highways moving among them.

Alan tripped on a stray loop of wire and, twisting, fell onto his back. He felt the sting of metal pierce his leg. Before he could get to his feet, the pursuer was on top of him, its tremendous weight crushing his body, a giant hand around his neck.

He clenched at the Brabillia's hand and threw a wild punch, but the attack produced no effect. In desperation, he threw strike after strike.

"Give it to me!" the creature shouted.

With all his effort, Alan tried to shift the attacker off, but the weight was too much for him.

Through the cacophony of clattering trash, the sound of steady thumping emerged. The two looked up the line to an approaching set of pile drivers.

"Give it to me!" the creature repeated in Alan's reddening face.

Alan reached into his jacket and pulled out the cylinder. He held it in front of their faces, then flung it over the edge of the belt down to the factory floor. The Brabillia looked to the crushers ahead, looked toward where the cylinder had gone, and then looked at Alan. He let go of him, rose to his feet, and leapt off the belt.

The pounding of the pile drivers grew louder.

Alan winced as he struggled to his feet. The thin metal shaft on the conveyor was wet with his blood.

Just ahead of the pile drivers, passing under the belt, a catwalk was approaching. With little time to prepare, he flung himself off the belt and onto the walkway, tumbling onto its unforgiving metal railings.

He clambered to his feet and limped beneath the conveyor to an access door. As the door sealed behind him, the heat and roaring of the plant subsided.

Alan slid down against the metal wall. The air in the respirator was soupy, and he breathed long and hard until he could feel oxygen running through his blood again. His body ached, covered in ash and rust, and his clothes were torn and punctured.

He reached into his jacket and produced a small rectangle of red-and-blue metal.

It survived.

He tucked the object back into his pocket, then pulled out his hand computer. It showed he wasn't far from a hangar. His pursuer wouldn't be fooled for long, and it was time for a quick exit of Eleva.

"I'm coming up," Alan said.

"You still have it?"

"It's fine. I'm fine. We're both in one piece."

Just one last sprint.

* * *

In a high orbit over Eleva, the glimmering white silhouette of a deep-galaxy expedition ship silently disappeared into the shadow cast by the planet. The vessel was the long-term home to a handful of engineers and scientists who signed onto research missions far from the populated core of the galaxy.

On board the ship, the computer lab was brightly lit and packed with equipment. Robotic arms with needle-tipped probes, oil baths with cables running into wire harnesses — every device a researcher could use for making sense of alien technology. In the back of the lab, a tiny red-and-blue rectangle was mounted in a holding case with cables running to a console.

Three individuals stared at a diagnostic display mounted from the ceiling. A column of text crawled down the screen.

Alan, with fresh clothes and damp hair slicked back, opened the lab door and limped in. "No med-bot can hold me down."

As Alan shut the door, the figures turned from the display. Etsel was the center of the trio, flanked by a student assistant and a man Alan did not recognize. Etsel was dressed in the formal style common with executives back at the school. He aspired to lead the xenoarchaeology department and dressed the part. Alan did not have fantasies of a reliable desk job, so he dressed simply. The stranger in the group was clothed as formally as Etsel, but in the more colorful style found in the Core regions. His graying hair was well kept.

"Alan! It's good to see you on your feet again, but I'm hoping the medical system isn't going to complain to me you were supposed to stay in bed," Etsel said as Alan hobbled to the group. He put a hand on the stranger's shoulder. "Dr. Zu, let me introduce you to Dr. Alan, the man who was able to secure us this piece of history at great personal risk."

"I've heard a lot about you, Dr. Alan. I'm Mattia Zu, here on behalf of the Core Alliance Research branch. As soon as Etsel contacted me, I had my ship get here as fast as it could — which sometimes isn't fast enough."

Core Alliance Research branch? Alan thought. *What is the Alliance doing here?*

Etsel continued, "We were just speaking about the implications of this bit of the Seed puzzle you found. I was telling Dr. Zu about all the effort we've put into tracking this one down: three systems over five months."

"For an intact memory module from the Seed, it's worth it." Alan looked up at the diagnostic screen. The test harness had connected to the artifact and was reading raw data from the ancient device segment by segment.

"And Dr. Alan here pioneered the techniques to decode and transform the memory —"

"Oh, we're familiar with Dr. Alan's work back at the lab." Zu interrupted. "We've been following him since he found the very first Seed artifact, the L9 specimen. The techniques you used to decode L9 — we've been replicating those and developing a few of our own."

"That leads back to why Zu has joined us here," Etsel said. "To make the most of this new discovery, the university decided that it was safest to let the Core Alliance Research team take possession of the artifact."

"What?" Alan laughed and turned to meet eyes with Etsel. "We tracked this thing through the Cistla sector for months. Why's it going off to the Alliance? Why isn't it staying here in the lab or going back to the school?"

"The Alliance has a team ready to try some fresh approaches they've been developing. And for our effort, they are funding this expedition for another two quarters," said Etsel.

Alan's face flushed, and he stepped back for a moment. "You're serious?"

"It will be in expert hands, Dr. Alan," Zu said. "We'll be taking it to a secure facility for study."

Alan looked at Etsel, then Zu, then back to Etsel. "It's right here, ready to be worked on."

"Thank you, Alan. Thank you for getting this, and to your assistant for helping validate its completeness," Zu said, "but I have to take it now."

"So, that's it? It's going into a vault?" Alan said, anger taking form in his tone.

"It's going to Core Research Labs," Etsel said coldly.

"They don't publish their work, you know that. Everyone knows that. They're a military institution —"

"Not military," Zu corrected.

"It's an institution that doesn't share what they discover." Alan pointed to the artifact. "If this memory block holds information that advances our understanding of who the Seed civilization were and where they went, we'd be the last to find out."

Zu produced a black case from his pocket and opened the lid. He looked at the lab tech. "Could you please put it in the container?" The tech scooped the rectangular tab of metal from its cradle and lowered it into the case, ignoring the conversation occurring around him.

"This is incredible," Alan stammered. "I didn't expect this from... from..."

"Please," Etsel said, "do your best to understand there are things that have transpired that you are not aware of."

Zu closed the lid. "The Alliance has tremendous resources to—"

"I don't... I can't hear it," Alan interrupted.

Zu and Etsel exchanged glances.

"Etsel, give my regards to the captain. I'll contact you when I get back to the lab. Great work."

"Certainly." Etsel looked to the lab technician. "Please escort our guest to his ship."

Zu and the assistant left, leaving Alan and Etsel in the lab in stony silence. Alan held himself against the counter and looked at the empty cradle where the artifact had been.

What have I been used for?

"Alan, I don't know what to say. I didn't imagine you reacting --"

"You knew the entire time that this was going to the Alliance." He paused and looked at the floor in thought. "Why didn't the Alliance just send their own man to get the artifact? Why did you send me?"

"Well, for starters, you worked on the L9 specimen for years and then literally wrote the book on Seed tech. If someone tried to give us a fake, or the situation evolved down some path nobody could predict, there's no better person to deal with it than you."

"I didn't join you on this ship to run errands and get chased all over backwater planets. I joined because I *need* to understand the Seed. And I thought you did too."

Alan rubbed his brow in frustration.

"Research gets messy sometimes," Etsel said. "This ship, this expedition—it isn't cheap. If you want to explore the distant boundaries of knowledge, sometimes you cut deals to pay the way."

"What if I don't want to cut deals?"

Etsel leaned back against a table. "There is a place for you on this expedition. You know that. But if you can't handle how it's run, then I can return you to Denarii where you can go back to digging up relics by yourself."

The room was quiet.

"What's it going to be, Alan?"

Chapter 2
Artifact

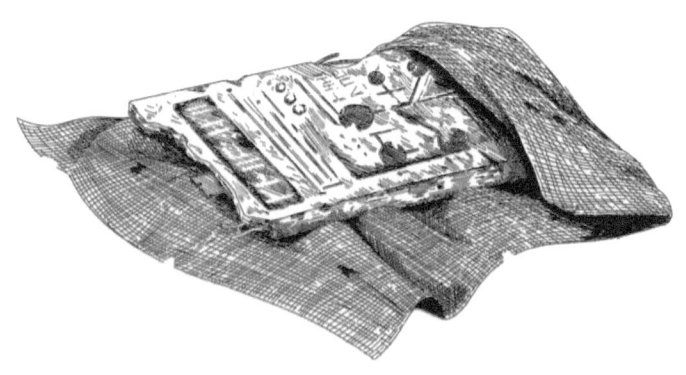

Three years later…

Despite the wet snow and coarse soil, Dr. Alan removed his gloves to feel the sharp edges of the stone ridge protruding from the ground. *Unmistakably sculpted by intelligent hands. How long has it been there, underneath all this?* Alan wiped away more of the muddy snow and dug ineffectively with tender fingers against the frozen soil. *Of course.*

He stood and put the gloves back on. Pointing to the ridge, he commanded a nearby labor-bot to carefully continue removing the frozen soil.

Snow was still falling into the pit that Dr. Alan shared with his robot and on the city that surrounded them. White frost blanketed the sidewalks that bordered his hole, the buildings that bordered the sidewalks, skyscrapers that overlooked it all. A tiny archaeological dig among city streets.

"Dr. Alan?" A young man's voice called from above the pit. Dr. Alan turned and found his face level with the man's shoes. He looked up and didn't recognize the figure.

"You a student?" Alan asked as he removed his face cloth and goggles.

"No, no," the man said. "I mean, unofficially, I am a student of yours. I read your books."

"So, not a student." Alan turned to watch the robot as he re-affixed his goggles and face cloth.

"When I was told to look for you here, I didn't expect to see this. I mean—" The young man gestured to the pit. "This is a little below where I thought you'd be."

Alan turned to the man. "And you are?"

"Mup. Mup—" he said, leaning down and extending a gloved hand.

"Mup, you're terrible with introductions. I don't think—"

"You are *the* expert on the Seed civilization. No one else even comes close. And you're on Denarii, digging a latrine," Mup chided with a smile.

"Mup—" Alan narrowed his eyes. "I don't know who you are. Can you get out of my site?"

Mup laughed and looked around the pit. "That's ambiguous. Do you want me out of your sight—or out of your *site*?"

"I don't care how you interpret it; it's the same to me. Get out."

"Sure. But—" Mup jumped into the pit, dug a gloved hand into his jacket pocket, and produced a flat, cloth-wrapped object. "This thing,"—he began to unwrap it—"traveled thirty light-years with me to get here—to get to you. Before that, who knows—millions of years in the ground, waiting to be discovered. And before that..."

Alan hesitated. He moved his goggles to his forehead and pulled down his face cloth again. He looked at the object in Mup's hands, lying bare on its cloth. He had never seen it before, but it was familiar. Its pattern of red and blue metals, finely etched lines, and a small unique script were instantly recognizable.

Mup shoved the object into Alan's hands.

Alan flipped the metal slab on all of its axes. He felt its weight, lightly bouncing it in his hands. Thin, but dense and strong. He took it over to the tiny stool that occupied a corner of the cramped pit. Removing both gloves, Alan felt the surfaces of the object with his bare fingers before placing it at the base of the lamp to see it better.

"Where did you get this?" Alan asked, transfixed by the object.

Mup walked the perimeter of the pit, inspecting the strata of soil. "I don't know. I found it while surveying a system for SEC—"

"And they didn't tell you where you were. So, you couldn't sell knowledge about the system to rock poachers."

Mup turned, eyebrows raised. "Oh? I didn't know you had been SEC."

"I wasn't—but in the past I worked with a lot who were."

Mup turned his attention to the labor-bot that was carefully plying away frozen soil from the stone ridge. "I see you got a robot doing your dirty work."

Alan ignored him and observed the way the artifact refracted the light that fell through it.

"I love messing with these guys," Mup said, as he tapped the robot on the head. The robot stopped its digging and turned to face Mup. Its bold, round, green-lit eyes turned to yellow expectantly. "Watch," Mup commanded the robot. Alan continued, ignoring them both.

Mup produced a silver coin from his pocket. He held it up in front of the robot's eyes so it could clearly observe the details of the disc. He rotated it between his fingers slowly, and with a sudden flick, he spread both of his hands out, palms up. The disc was gone.

"Where'd it go?" Mup asked with a smile. "Where'd the coin go? You don't know." The robot stared at each of Mup's hands, silently bouncing its gaze between each. "He doesn't know. Can't figure it out, bucket o' bolts."

The robot stiffened, its eyes lifting to focus straight ahead. A fault light illuminated on the robot's shoulder, and the robot announced, "Running self-check."

Mup laughed. "It gets them every time."

Alan was still hunched over the object — observing it. Mup walked behind him and crouched to look over his shoulder.

"So," Mup asked, wisps of condensation following his words, "I've got this thing, this clue — and I want to go with you, the famous Dr. Alan, to figure out where it came from — where it leads to."

Alan stopped rubbing the metal. He grabbed the cloth off the stool and wrapped the object back up.

The two stood and faced each other.

Alan pushed the wrapped object back into Mup's hands. "No. That's not me anymore."

Mup's expectant smile faded. "You're Dr. Alan, right? The Dr. Alan who would drop everything and go to the frontiers at the slightest smell of a clue to the Seed civilization?"

"That's not me anymore. There are others — more capable, better funded. I don't chase the Seed's ghosts like I used to. And," Alan sighed, "if I did, I work alone."

"I don't—I don't understand. Is it this?" Mup asked, holding up the cloth-shrouded bundle. "It's pretty clear. I mean, am I wrong?"

Alan took a deep breath. "This isn't my thing now," he said, shaking his head. "You should go."

Mup stared at Alan, hoping for a change in Alan's face that did not arrive. "Okay," Mup said as he pushed the object into his pocket. He rubbed the back of his neck. "Can I give you my contact—"

"No. You can go." Alan put his goggles and gloves back on. "I'm sure the university can find someone for you. You know where they are."

* * *

The evening had fallen, and the snow had not stopped. In another hour, snow would begin accumulating faster than Alan or the labor-bot could keep up with. Alan attached a utility cable to the bot and threw a tarp over the figure.

"See you tomorrow," he said to the robot, knowing it did not care.

He stepped out onto the frozen sidewalk and locked the gate behind him.

Alan's apartment was not far from the site. It was ten minutes of walking through the city's narrow gullies, where skyscrapers parted just enough for the citizens to roam. Figures wrapped in heavy clothing walked in pairs, arm-in-arm in case they slipped, and in every direction. As they passed Alan, he could overhear the foreign tongues, the private conversations, the random staccato of a sudden laugh with no context echoing over the buildings.

Despite the weather, the biting cold, and the ceaseless snow, the passing figures exuded peaceful contentment.

Contentment on a narrow island in a wide sea, far from any other island, on a planet that itself was an island far from any other. A frontier planet whose existence and utility were owed to being near nothing else.

The city was young with students and frontier officials. There was no native population, at least none that was not the subject of an archaeological dig. Everyone was an immigrant, coming from somewhere else. Alan was from somewhere else.

Alan's mind worked over the object as he walked through trodden snow. It was an incredible specimen — the biggest one he had ever seen himself. Most of the Seed artifacts he had come across were smaller, but more importantly, not of any intrinsic value. They were often small pieces of something bigger — but not a valuable part of that bigger thing. The skin of a ship, a connecting rod. The piece Mup had brought... it was part of...

He had found a similar specimen early in his search. It was only the size of a fingernail, but it had been an unending spring of knowledge and insight on the Seed civilization. Specimen L9. It was a computing device piggybacked on solid-state memory. Alan had spent three years studying it. He had become more familiar with that single square centimeter of material than anyone else had with anything that small. He had written two books on it and given presentations to thousands of students and scientists.

Mup's piece was like L9 — but a hundred times larger. A far more complete piece.

A thought leapt into his mind before he could think it away: *Why did I say no?*

Restaurants were emptying, the steam on the windows disappearing, behind which labor-bots cleared empty tables. Flashing signs flickered off one by one. The voices of pedestrians got increasingly distant as Alan turned into the alley that led to his apartment.

The door to the building clicked open as Alan approached. He gasped and held his breath as he ran through the lobby, exhaling sharply when he reached the stairwell. The lobby had smelled like rotten soo-flower for weeks, but the tenants had been unable to convince the labor-bots (who could not smell) to fix it.

Up seven flights of stairs, through another door, Alan arrived at his apartment. The hallway carpet was soggy from snow packed into the soles of shoes.

With a gentle click, the door unlocked and opened, and Alan went in, shutting the door behind him.

The sound of excited feet running across tile filled the apartment as his robotic pet leapt from the couch to find Alan's ankles. He smiled and petted the little creature. Its synthetic hair changed color from brown to bright blue, and its tail wagged furiously. It rolled onto its back and spread its three legs so Alan could rub the creature's chest.

"All right, all right. Calm down."

It had been a gift he'd received many years prior, and although he hadn't felt particularly strong about it, he could never bring himself to give it away. Now the little creature was the soul of the apartment.

"Make something warm," Alan asked the home chef computer as he passed by on his way to the shower. "Nothing too fancy."

He threw his wet clothing into the hamper and walked naked into the warm, orange, aromatic mists already spraying in the glass cabinet of his shower.

Alan thought over the artifact, replaying in his mind how it had looked and felt.

The L9 artifact had kept Alan busy for years, and near the end, when he had unlocked the methods for extracting information from the artifact's registers, it had led to years of research work for anthropologists, linguists, and computer scientists. They had pored over the recovered data — but it was not enough to lead to the origin of the Seed civilization.

Mup's artifact would be transformative. Not only did it have magnitudes greater potential storage, but if the data recovered was from a navigation system or an encyclopedic databank —

What if there were more? What if there were a million more under Mup's feet when he had found it?

Alan stopped the shower.

The techniques used on L9, the lessons learned from the resultant data — all could be reused to speed up research and exploitation. Whoever completed the data extraction process... *Whoever.*

Alan sat down. He felt his stomach turn.

In his mind, Alan imagined Mup walking into a strange science office, placing the wrapped object on an examination table. The scientist would be skeptical but polite. Mup would unwrap the cloth, and the scientist would be disbelieving. And then, they would recognize what they were looking at — and the magnitude of what had arrived at their table. Would they try to cut Mup out? It did not matter.

They would probe Mup's story for clues, analyze the artifact for hints to its origin — figuring out where it came from would lead them to more.

Then they would fly back to the spot where Mup had found it. Just underneath the first layer of dirt, they would uncover more artifacts.

Back in the lab, they would use the techniques and systems that Alan had pioneered to bring the ancient technology back to life. Awakening the artifact, they would catch the lake of secrets it spilled out, a priceless trove of knowledge on the most elusive secret in the galaxy.

It would start with news spreading out to the other systems. A breakthrough. The scientist would travel to the Core worlds to present at the Core Alliance Anthropology and Archaeology Symposium. They would keynote. Afterward, they would tour like celebrities through galas and donor events, courted by the elite from a hundred systems, all of whom offered more funding than he could use.

Awards. Achievement. Recognition.

All of it on the shoulders of my work.

Alan felt his hearing go hollow and his eyes lose color. His head slumped to his shoulder, and he fell to his side, lying on the warm wet tile of the shower.

After a moment, he regained his senses and sat up. Alan called to the apartment computer, "Get me a registry of ships that recently arrived in the system."

Chapter 3
Mup

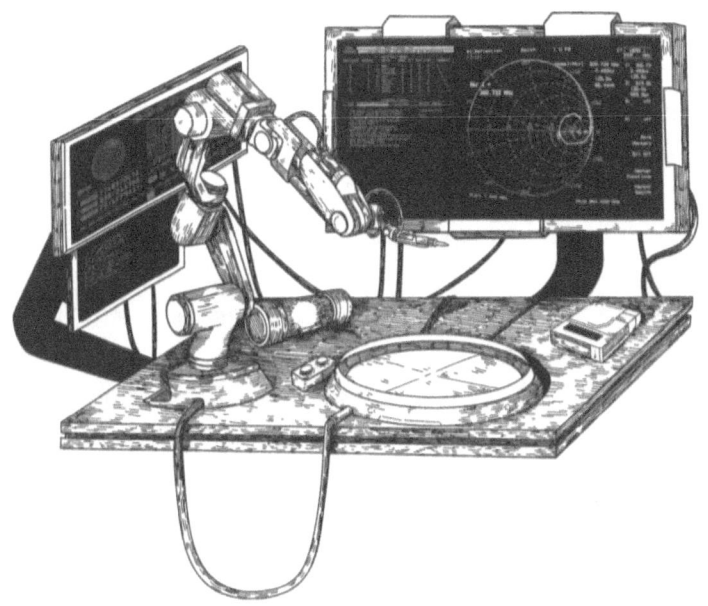

Mup emerged from his apartment, turning to make sure the door didn't close before he checked the pockets of his cold coat. Satisfied he hadn't forgotten anything, he took his foot from the door and began covering his neck and face with the wrap his mother had given him before he left for Denarii. Even though it had been years, the wrap still had the smell of home, and every time he put it on, it triggered a memory of green hills and family. He smiled to himself.

Denarii was far from his family home, and certainly different, but Mup wasn't here often enough for it to feel like anything other than a place to sleep and store his things. Even the ships he frequented for work did not feel like home — a true home.

The elevator sensed Mup's approach and automatically called for the car. As Mup waited, he recalled the errands to be done. Bathroom supplies, food, appointments...

The elevator chimed, and the doors opened. Dr. Alan stepped out.

"Do you still have the artifact?" Alan asked.

Mup's shock was visible in his wide eyes and on his raised brows. He quickly pulled the wrap from around his mouth. "Dr. Alan?"

Alan grabbed Mup's elbow firmly and repeated, "Do you still have the artifact?"

"Yes, but..." Mup struggled. "How did you find me?"

"These are things I'm good at," Alan said coldly. "Is it in your apartment?"

"Of course, but..."

"Good, what number? Let's go see about it," Alan said as he pulled Mup down the hall.

"Have you just been riding the elevator waiting for me?" Mup asked with disbelief.

Alan didn't answer.

* * *

Alan's lab was small but well utilized. Every shelf was covered in metal instruments, glass-jarred specimens, unrecognizable technical gadgets or coiled wires. Cabinets under the counter space, each labeled meticulously, lined every wall. White light from the snowy cityscape filtered in from the windows.

Alan had the artifact on a steel examination table on the center island. A pair of metal arms attached to the island held out an array of instruments and cabling, which Alan occasionally accepted as he probed the artifact with various lights and gizmos.

Mup walked the periphery, inspecting the lab closely — not hesitating to turn an object so he could see it better.

"What changed your mind?" Mup asked as he ran his hand over a wooden box. "You seemed really certain back at the latrine."

"I think best in the shower."

Mup could sense in Alan's tone, in his urgency earlier to get back to the lab, that more had changed than a shower.

"Let's hook this in and see what we can see," Alan said. Mup wasn't sure if it was meant for him, or a habit Alan had of thinking out loud. "Maybe it won't fight us."

Mup leaned in and focused on a gold triangular form on a shelf. "What's this for?"

"Ninety-five percent of the things I have in here I don't need very often. But…" Alan paused to push a resistant cable into place, resuming when it snapped affirmatively. "When you do need it, it's all the difference if you have it."

"It must have cost a lot."

Alan ignored him. "What do you remember about the system?"

"Where I got the artifact?"

"No, where you met your mother."

Mup passed over the jab. "At first it wasn't remarkable, until it was," Mup said as Alan continued to fidget with uncooperative wiring. "One star. Warm. A number of uninhabitable planets, but two very habitable — which is why we were there. We had to do a quick anthro survey of the habitables because they were about to be destroyed."

"What?" Alan asked, looking to Mup.

"Yeah. The system was on a survey list for a long time, but last year the know-alls back in the Core realized the two habitables were going to collide. They had us rush in and do some quick surveys before it got all smashed up — destroyed." Mup knocked his fists together.

"That *is* interesting," Alan remarked. "When's the big event?"

"Two weeks." Mup sighed as he continued sorting through the shelf contents. "And it takes a week to get there."

"I wish you had led with that detail." He paused and thought for a moment. "That complicates things, but, not impossible, I suppose." Alan returned his attention to the artifact and the diagnostic cabling.

Mup continued, "We were there, I was there, for anthropological research. We knew there was a primitive intelligent civilization on the green habitable, so I was supposed to set up equipment to document a village for future study."

"For after they were gone," Alan said.

"When I was with the villagers, that's when I got the artifact."

"From the villagers?"

"Yeah. They were a pretty basic tribe. Wood and fire. The artifacts stuck out. The tribe wasn't capable of making anything that resembled the Seed stuff."

Alan stood and looked to Mup. "So, there is more?"

"A lot more."

"How much is 'a lot more'?"

"They-were-eating-off-them more."

Alan's eyebrows lifted. "That is a lot." He looked to the artifact. "Was this a dinner plate?"

Mup laughed. "No, that was tied to a tree, and I traded them a comb for it."

Alan surfaced a laugh. "Wow."

"Yeah, it'll make sense when you get there." Mup turned back to the shelves.

Satisfied that his cabling was in place, Alan took a small cylinder from the mechanical arms and twisted its top so that a bright light emitted from the other end. He ran the light up and down the artifact and watched a monitor mounted from the ceiling.

"All right. One star and at least two habitables," Alan dictated to his computer.

"Two habitable for sure, maybe ten uninhabitable," Mup added.

"… and maybe 10 uninhabitable. Distance of twenty-seven to thirty-two light-years. And this spectrographic signature." With theatrical embellishment, Alan placed the cylinder into a fitted receptacle and pushed a blue confirmation button. "Send it off to the computer. It cross-checks the system registry. Results in three minutes. Hopefully we'll know where it was you traded a comb for this," Alan finished.

Alan watched as Mup continued moving down the shelf silently, thoroughly inspecting each item.

Alan broke the silence. "You see that over there?"

Mup followed Alan's gaze to a small metal case with glass shelving, then walked over to it and opened the glass, pulling out a small, clear box. Contained inside, a small fragment of torn red and blue metal with intricate etchings — no bigger than a fingernail.

"That is L9," Alan said.

Mup held the container close to his eyes. He turned it gently between his fingers. "Unbelievable," he said softly. "I read your books. You worked for years on this."

Alan folded his arms and spoke with pride. "That's right. That piece of Seed kept me busy, day and night, for years. Entire facilities all around the Core, busy for years too."

Alan turned to Mup's artifact, put his hands on either side of the examination tray, and leaned in to get a close view of the artifact's details.

"And this," he said, "this artifact, you found tied to a tree — it eclipses L9 in every way."

Mup turned to Alan.

"But," Alan continued, "more importantly, we could never trace where L9 came from because L9 was missing its *you*."

Mup thought about the implications. Without himself, the artifact's origin would be a mystery.

"The spectro profile of this artifact matches a thousand systems, but with the details you provided, we can narrow it down, and if the computer tells us where you found this... it's a totally different game."

Alan stood back up. "We have never seen the pieces *together*, just isolated fragments. Just single pieces of the puzzle. If we found a complete Seed wreck or a Seed settlement, it could reveal the clues that lead back to..."

"... the Seed civilization's home world," Mup finished.

"That's right, the genesis of it all. The civilization that started all other civilizations." Alan paused and looked out the window. "If we found their home, imagine what we could learn about the galaxy and ourselves."

Mup looked at L9, then put it back in its case.

"As soon as we know where this piece came from —" Alan mimed a ship shooting off into space. "Get a ship, a few labor-bots, fly out, collect what can be collected, then get off-world and watch the fireworks."

The computer chimed completion. "System located with near certainty: H19-98."

"And there we have it," Alan said, glancing up at the monitor. He began unplugging the connections to the exam table and artifact. "It's important I go to… aitch-one-nine-nine-eight… now and get what can be got before it's gone." Alan stopped and looked to Mup. "It's good you didn't tell anyone about this."

Mup was silent. Alan froze.

"It's good you didn't tell anyone about this," Alan repeated. "Please tell me no one else knows about this."

"I came to you first, and you clearly said no. You basically spit in my face, so —" Mup said with a rising edge of defiance.

"So, what did you do?"

"I went to the next person on my list. Zu."

Alan trembled, looking down to the table. A hand clenched his hair. "Oh, no." Alan grabbed the island and steadied himself. "Out of all the hucksters on this planet —"

"Hucksters?" Mup interrupted.

" — you go to… Zu. He's the worst person you could have taken this to," Alan said, raising his voice.

"No," Mup responded, "I can think of a lot of people worse than —"

"No, you can't," Alan interrupted. "Zu is an entirely unique blend of knowing *just* enough to trick people into trusting him and being well connected enough to have powerful people around him to trick. Everything he touches disappears into the labs of the Core Alliance." Alan walked to Mup, eyes fixed in an intense stare. "If Zu had gotten to that," — Alan pointed to L9 — "we'd only know what they wanted to share with us, which would be nothing."

"I told him what I told you," Mup shot back. "He looked at it with a scope, but that's it."

"He scanned it with a spectro," Alan said.

"A spec — ?" Mup asked, genuinely confused about what it was.

"A spectro," Alan said as he walked quickly back to the examination table and sifted through the mess of cables and instruments on the island. He found the spectro, plainly sitting in its rest. "This," he said holding the cylinder. "This is a spectro."

"Yes, one of those. A spectro." Mup gestured back, "I don't even know what that is."

"This tells me what elements are present on the artifact, what kind of star it was near, what kind of radiation it's been subject to," Alan continued. "And with your story..."

"He runs the same calculations you did," Mup realized.

"He runs the same calculations I did."

"He knows where I found it?" Mup asked.

Alan turned away and rubbed his head. "He's probably already on his way."

"So, we have to go," Mup said, standing tall.

"No, I have to go," Alan replied sternly. "Your part is already done."

Mup bristled and walked to the island, standing opposite Alan over the artifact. "No, my part is not already done. I did not bring this here to you so I could watch you blast off on an adventure. I'm going." Mup's voice tensed. "I'm the one who found it. I'm the one who brought it here and tried to convince you to take it on. It's my artifact —"

Alan's eyes locked on Mup's. "Is it? Is it *your* artifact?"

Mup realized he had stepped over an invisible line in Alan's ethics, triggering a violent eruption in the doctor's eyes.

"If you want this thing to live beyond a closed lab somewhere," Alan continued through tightly clenched teeth, "you need to rationalize this with yourself right now: who does history belong to? You, them, or everyone?"

There was silence as Mup thought about what Alan was asking.

"You and me... everyone," Mup replied.

Alan began to wrap up the artifact, but Mup placed a hand firmly on the slab of metal. "It *is* for everyone — but it delivered itself to me," he said slowly, keeping his eyes fixed on Alan's. "So, I go where it goes."

Alan and Mup held their stares. Alan could see the fire in Mup's face, barely veiled. The young man knew what he wanted, and Alan felt a twist of admiration.

Alan spoke slowly. "We have to go. Right now."

Mup's lips curled. "We have to go. Right now."

Chapter 4

Helios

Two colorful jewels of planets floated in the pitch black of space. One, an opulent green sea of jungle with smatterings of dazzling blue lakes over which smears of white clouds loomed—the other, a foreboding dark mass of greenish-blue oceans with specks of snow-covered islands. The ocean planet hid behind its sister, unusually close, obscured in the eclipsing shadow of its sibling.

A blip of intense light in the darkness of space signaled a ship returning to sublight speed. The approaching vessel, a small arrowhead-shaped scout, fired its forward thrusters to slow its dramatic plunge toward the green planet.

Inside, the two occupants clambered into their seats in the cramped cockpit and strapped themselves in for entry into the atmosphere. The hibernation pods, mounted vertically behind the seats, sealed themselves and powered off—their job completed.

"There they are. Aren't they beautiful? I knew I'd be back," Mup sighed, looking out the viewport as he pulled floating restraints to bear around his shoulders.

Alan's eyes were heavy, the effect of the hibernation drugs wearing off. "I haven't flown in a while. I forgot how rough it is."

"Rough indeed. But better than a week of sitting in these chairs, trying to make conversation, wouldn't you say?" Mup replied as he stretched his legs below the console.

"I think we agree."

"Well, the ship isn't too bad. I'm curious how you got it so fast," Mup said, finally settled into his restraints.

Alan searched the ceiling control panel for a vent. "The university keeps a few on hand." He found the vent and twisted it for maximum air. "We were lucky it was available. But don't go thinking it was free."

"Oh?"

"I put a few thousand down to guarantee we'd bring it back in good shape," Alan said, rubbing sweat off his forehead.

"You look terrible." Mup smiled at Alan.

Alan started to respond but realized Mup was probably right. Hibernation didn't wear well on someone who hadn't done it in a while—and Alan was getting older too.

"What are they named?" Alan asked.

Mup was confused. "Aitch-one… I forget —"

"No, no. When you surveyed them. What did you call them?" Alan gestured to the planets. "Nobody ever calls them by their registry."

"Oh. Helios, for where we are going, and Ceto for the ocean one. Sibling planets," Mup said, watching the worlds get larger. "And I called the natives of Helios the Heliops."

"Creative," Alan remarked.

"Better than 'rats'. The Heliops look like huge rats."

The ship's autopilot chimed an alarm and asked for further direction.

"Tell me where to take her," Alan said, keeping his eyes on the computer.

"Get us in a regular route along the equator. We'll be looking for a large green crater, and then we'll land near the center."

"There is so much green down there, it looks like it might be all trees," Alan said as he punched in arrival orders to the computer.

"It is all trees," Mup said.

"All trees?" Alan's eyebrow raised.

"All trees. They grow up a full mile. They are so tall, you can't see the surface when you look down, just a green abyss. It took a long time to find a safe place to land, which is why we'll end up in the same spot as before."

"Anything to watch out for?" Alan asked, looking up from the computer.

"Birds. Very, very big birds."

The ship skipped through the upper atmosphere, its dive shallow, so that Mup and Alan fully orbited the planet along its belt before arriving back at their intended destination, a hundred miles east of a large green crater. Their relative speed slowed dramatically; Alan kicked on the forward thrusters again to commit the ship into Helios's gravity.

The sound of wind-noise filled the vessel as the atmosphere thickened. Alan assumed control from the autopilot and guided the ship over the great eastern wall of the crater, crossing a mile above its crest. The rim of the crater loomed thousands of feet over the jungle canopy — but even as high as it was, the ridge of the crater was equally covered in trees as the crater floor far below. Currents of air flowing over the wall lifted the ship up suddenly, then dropped off as they passed over, leaving the ship in mega-vortices of turbulent air.

Accelerating through the turbulence, Alan dropped the ship closer to the jungle canopy, which rushed underneath as they zipped over the treetops. Alan could sense the proportions and age of the mega-foliage. Thousands of small birds, specks of lively color, emerged and disappeared in great flocks into the trees all around — out to the horizon.

"Not so low, not so fast," Mup said, gesturing with his hand to rise. "It'll be hard to spot the entrance to the landing zone from down here — and you want to stay away from — "

An enormous gray bird, far greater in size than the ship, swept into the viewport, flying directly in the ship's path. Alan instinctively pulled back hard, and the ship shot up, flattening Mup and Alan into their seats. Alan pushed forward, and both fell tight against their restraints. They had gained enough altitude to be as high as the crater walls.

Alan gave Mup a sideways glance.

"There, you can see it now." Mup leaned forward, pointing. "That's where I landed last time."

Alan scanned the horizon. *So much life!* he thought as he continued searching. *What can support all of this?*

Then Alan saw the break in the canopy. It was a quarter-mile in diameter, a column of clearing in the otherwise-unrelenting jungle canopy.

Mup spoke. "It had to be from a small meteorite a few years ago. The jungle is so thick, not an inch of space to spare without a struggle. There is really no other place to land around here."

"Certainly."

Alan slowed the ship as it approached the break and circled it in a bank to bleed off the remaining inertia. He looked out the side viewport and saw down the vertical column cut into the jungle. Thick, green foliage, occasionally broken by tremendous branches of light wood that pierced out, covered the throat of the shaft and disappeared down into a dark green abyss like Mup had described. Flocks of birds shot out into the light and disappeared again. Solo birds with tremendous wingspans loitered above the mouth of the space, staying aloft with warm currents billowing out from the surface like a chimney. Within the column, smaller birds swirled in circles, following the perimeter of the column.

"There! Heliops!" Mup shouted excitedly with a finger pointed toward the nose of the ship.

Alan followed Mup's finger and saw only three large birds skimming slowly over the tops of the canopy far ahead. He was about to ask what Mup meant when he realized there were figures *on* the birds. Alan squinted.

"Are the Heliops—riding the birds?"

"It's incredible! Yes, they ride them to travel to other villages," Mup said with glee. Alan smiled to himself.

Alan leveled the vessel from its turn and slowed it to hover over the lip of the column. "All right, let's go in," Alan said as he pulled a set of glasses from the ceiling panel. He unfolded them and put them on. A tiny light showed to Mup that the glasses were operating, giving Alan a view through the hull of the ship to get an unobstructed perspective of the surroundings. Alan looked into his lap as he guided the ship vertically down into the hole in the canopy.

Mup touched his display panel so he could view the feed from Alan's perspective.

Mup leaned forward to get a closer look at the panel. "It's a few hundred feet down; we're looking for a flat, wide limb."

Alan's head scanned below the ship, searching for the branch. There were many, but nearly all were clearly unable to support a landing vessel.

"There, that's it," Mup said. "You were just looking at it. Yes, that one in the center of your vision. It…"

They both paused.

Alan said, "It has a ship on it."

Alan continued guiding the vessel toward the large, uneven platform. There were branches of all sizes jutting out, obscuring the landing area and making it difficult to approach directly. Alan slowed the descent and slid the ship back to navigate around a cluster of vine-covered branches that blocked his path.

"Watch it, there are some more off to our right," Mup called. He caught a glimpse of a large, hairless, green monkey with yellow platters for eyes before it squinted, leapt to another branch, and swung into the chaos of vines and leaves.

As they weaved closer to the landing area, they could see humanoids walking near the ship. They had a small pile of crates off to the side away from the exposed end of the massive branch.

Mup broke the tension as he pushed the landing gear lever forward, "Dropping the gear." Four mechanical thuds indicated the landing bays opening. All four of the indicator lights turned amber, then individually green.

"They didn't leave a lot of room for anyone else," Mup observed as he watched Alan guide the ship down from the monitor.

"Zu never does," Alan replied.

"Going to be tight."

Zu's ship rose into sight through the viewports as Alan moved the scout down next to it. He held the ship in a hover a few inches above the branch and carefully touched down, testing the branch to see if it could accommodate more weight. Satisfied, Alan dropped the throttle to five percent, then cut it off completely.

Through the viewport, Mup could see the figures were human — a handful of men who looked like the sort that made a living running ships out to uncharted systems. Young, clearly in good shape, dressed for work that required getting dirty. But one figure was different. An older man with thick, white hair, watching Mup's ship and directing the younger men to clear equipment near it.

Alan shut down the ship and unlocked his restraints. Mup checked the ceiling panel for any warning lights, then unrestrained himself as well.

"Looks hot," Alan said as he opened his utility closet.

"It's *really* hot here. But keep a jacket—the heat is insufferable, but the plants are worse," Mup replied as he grabbed a coat from the closet. "Also, keep a gun ready—always."

"That was my line," Alan said as he watched Mup pull out his belt holster.

"The gun isn't for Zu. It's for the creatures. There is a lot that wants to eat you here."

"You underestimate Zu's appetite," Alan replied with a sly grin.

Alan moved to the back of the ship. He reached the starboard bulkhead and pulled the mechanical door-lock lever down, triggering a warning light. He reached down, lifted the ratchet sliding door up, and locked it into its open position. A chorus of foreign bird songs filled the cockpit, followed by a rolling wave of broiling, humid heat—and the smell of rotting wood and mold.

Alan stood in the ship's door and surveyed the jungle looming overhead. Birds near and far exchanged rhythmic chirping coos and whoops, keeping pitched song over a steady chorus of droning buzzes. Above Alan, but out of sight, something whistled with a long warbling song, its notes hollow but confident. A chaotic mosaic of tree leaves shrouded most everything except large tree limbs that emerged and then disappeared back into the sea of green. The breeze circulating within the shaft kept the trees and fronds swaying and shimmering constantly, making any creatures movements lost in the noise.

Sunlight, blasting down the shaft from above, took the form of an intense yellow beam that turned creatures flying in the open into flares of light.

A hard insect flew wildly at Alan, smacking solidly into his chest, bumbling loudly, then flew off into the canopy.

Many years on Denarii had led Alan to forget the sounds and smells of intense nature that a jungle provided.

Amazing, he thought as all his senses tingled from the unfamiliar environment.

"Alan!"

Alan broke from his trance to see the older man call out to him, waving with a smile. Another taller man stood behind, unmoved by the new arrivals.

Alan jumped down from the ship onto the branch and sensed the massive limb's unshakeable anchor to its parent trunk.

"Zu," Alan replied slowly as he walked to the man.

Mup appeared in the ship's doorway, a rifle cradled in his arms.

"Alan! I'm glad you could join us," Zu shouted as Alan continued toward him. Zu offered a hand and waited for Alan, who, when he was close enough, took Zu's hand.

"So glad you could join us," Zu repeated with a broad smile as the two held outstretched hands, "but this spot is taken!"

Alan could see Zu and his companion were drenched in sweat. Alan could feel the sweat, the humidity, beginning to stick to his own brow. He didn't reply or smile but instead held Zu's hand and locked eyes.

Zu continued, "But no worry, there are other beautiful places in the galaxy to dig!"

"It's good to see you, Zu," Alan said with a reserved tone. Alan politely shook Zu's hand once, then let go.

"Simply fantastic, isn't it!" Zu said as he looked toward the mouth of the shaft. "Tremendous — but a shame the planet will be obliterated soon." Zu watched Alan for a reaction.

"Your companion, we haven't met," Alan said as he reached out to the man looming behind Zu. He was tall and young — but his skin showed the signs of frequent exposure to hostile environments. The man must have been well-traveled.

"Oh, I think you've probably met at some point. This is Tier. He has been my guide for some time." Zu smiled.

Tier accepted Alan's hand in a firm handshake.

"I didn't know you kept anyone longer than one term," Alan remarked as he turned to his own ship. "That's Mup. He was the target of your most recent con." Alan pointed to Mup, who stood watching in the doorway.

Mup, sensing he was being introduced, waved from the door.

Zu laughed. "We've met. Charming kid." Zu got close to Alan and put a familial arm around his shoulder. "But really, you must be going. I told the Core Alliance we'd be in and out and we'd bring no more people than absolutely necessary. You wouldn't imagine the trouble you'll get into if they hear about you—"

"Mup and I will be staying for a bit," Alan interrupted as he walked away from Zu's hold. "Finish up some work I began."

An animal screeched wildly above, and a branch of leaves shook. Another screech, this time in another voice from the same set of branches. An obscured struggle shook the branches violently for a quick moment before a green monkey swung out from the scene and leapt to a nearby branch. It turned to hiss toward the set of leaves from which it had emerged.

"The natives are territorial," Alan said, looking up to the trees. "You'll fit right in!" he finished, flashing a forced smile.

"Alan," Zu began, following behind Alan, "it's impossible for you to stay. Frankly, we have the rights from the Core Alliance to work in this system, and I really must insist you leave. For safety's sake. We cannot be doing our work and watching you. Why don't we catch up afterward?"

"No, Zu." Alan turned. "You know I also have rights from the university to attend to significant archaeological events. This one is pretty significant," Alan said. He mimed two planets colliding and the subsequent explosion with his fists.

Zu ruffed his hair. "It's been three years. Three years since you went quiet on Seed research and stopped publishing."

"Well, I've been busy."

"With what, exactly?" Zu's smile had disappeared.

Alan turned to survey the landing area. Zu's ship was larger; it could carry enough cargo to necessitate a landing ramp. Most of Zu's four crew were unloading the last of a few crates — stacking them forty yards down the landing limb under the shadowy cover of the green foliage of the shaft walls. A single crewmember remained in the hold to return cargo netting to its storage. Tier shadowed Zu, silently observing the conversation.

"The usual," said Alan. "But I'm most excited about a recent development. I have no doubt you'll be reading about it later."

Zu sighed. "Alan, I know you, and I know how important your work was to you. But since you disappeared," Zu paused, "our understanding of the Seed civilization has evolved. The work I've done, the work the lab has done, has led to new understanding and new meaning." Alan looked to Zu. "The Core Alliance doesn't want you to get in the way." Zu glanced at Tier.

Tier produced a computer pad, swiped the screen, and selected a page. He handed it to Alan.

"Anyone not in my expedition is forbidden from being in the system — specifically…"

Alan looked up from the pad.

"… *you*," Zu emphasized.

"Alan!" Mup called with hesitation from the ship.

Alan ignored Mup. "Then the Core Alliance can bring me to the board when I get back," he said, shoving the pad into Zu's arms.

Tier stepped in reverse and unholstered his pistol, raising it to his hip. Zu paused a moment and stepped back.

"Alan, they are serious — "

"No — quiet!" Tier hissed.

Zu and Alan both froze.

A rush of bird wings flapping trembled through the air, flocks of birds flying in a twirling swarm upward in the light out of the shaft. The songs and whistles of the jungle were absent.

Tier looked to the crew near the jungle wall and flashed a hand-sign. The crew, without hesitation, began climbing into the branches of the jungle.

"Something is not right," Tier stressed.

Zu sprinted to his ship, surprising Alan with his spryness. The crewman in the cargo hold, sensing the sudden change, had already produced a rifle, which he tossed to Zu. Alan felt naked.

Alan saw Mup running from the ship with a rifle in each hand. "You never know with this place," Mup cautioned as he gave Alan the extra weapon.

Tier and Zu retreated slowly from the edges of the landing area. Mup and Alan, in their own pair, kept their distance but paced Tier.

Among the flurry and beating of bird wings, a different sound began to fill the jungle: tremendous claps of wood cracking, whooshes of leaves shaking violently, and the deep drone of a nefarious buzzing.

The swarm of birds ended, disappearing into the open sky.

A single bug as large as a child emerged, flying wildly without direction or purpose. It twirled toward Alan and Mup, buzzing louder and louder as it anxiously looped. The whirring of its wings split through the air.

Mup drew his pistol and struggled to keep it focused on the bug.

Another buzzing black lump emerged from the shaft.

And another.

And then a swarm.

Mup cracked off two shots at the first bug as it swung wildly through the air, finally diving toward Alan. The last shot hit the creature, blasting a wing off in a shower of black, spiny plates and wet chunks of fibrous flesh. It crashed into the ground and slid toward Alan, slashing wildly with its assembly of sickly legs, trying desperately to taste blood.

Alan, without hesitation, lowered his rifle toward the bug as it flipped and whirled wildly toward him. He fired, triggering a tremendous blast. The spot where it had been exploded in a blinding blast of flying wood shrapnel and fiery debris.

Both Mup and Alan found themselves lying on their backs, stunned by the explosion. Alan struggled to get to a knee by the time Mup reached him.

Covered in sooty debris and wood chips, Alan looked to Mup, wide-eyed. "Why do they keep cannons in that ship?"

"Get up." Mup lifted Alan to his feet. "There's more!"

Tier began shooting with a pistol toward the swarm as it swirled slowly toward the group of men.

Mup, with Alan in tow, ran to Tier and Zu.

"Get to the trees!" Tier shouted. "Follow —"

The group froze.

From the depth of the jungle shaft, an enormous tentacle of red flesh covered in spines and nodules, surrounded by clouds of swarming bugs, snaked up toward the sky. Writhing and whirling, the tentacle touched a thick branch, and a pulse of bright blue swept up and down the arm. Triggered by blind reflex, the horrid arm coiled around the branches near it — like a monster vine latching on to the surrounding jungle — and stiffened.

"This will be interesting," Mup blurted over the cacophony of buzzing, his eyes fixed on the tentacle.

Chapter 5

Monsters

A nother tentacle shot across the jungle shaft and similarly tangled itself in foliage. Then another and another, until there were uncountable arms pulling at the jungle.

The swarm of flying black bugs twirled through the air like a tornado. The ominous cloud creeped closer to the group until the creatures flew blindly into the ships' hulls, smacking and splattering like nightmarish bits of fleshy hail.

The insects that survived their suicidal flight flopped around where they landed, spraying yellow glops of fluid from broken wings or legs.

As if sensing the bugs' excitement, a nearby tentacle released its hold on the jungle trees and whipped wildly until it contacted the limb on which the ships rested. The arm swung itself so that it wrapped once around the limb, over both of the ships. Sensing its grip, the tentacle tightened and yanked downward.

The entire limb jerked down, colossal snaps within the interior of the limb shooting shock waves up to the group's feet and moving the limb so it angled down ominously. Both ships shifted toward the abyss of the shaft.

Mup hipshot his rifle toward a bridge of tentacle between the two ships but missed, clearing a swath of bugs behind it in a blast of fiery plasma.

"To the trees!" Zu cried.

Tier led the charge away from the ships.

Mup grabbed Alan's arm as he turned to run and held him back. "The ship!"

"Forget the ship—"

"No!" Mup shouted. "*Their* ship!"

Alan looked beyond Mup and saw the tentacle had tightened around both ships and collapsed their landing gear. In the cargo bay of Zu's ship, the sole crewman gripped the wall in fear.

Mup bolted toward the craft, dodging an errant black flying blob.

"Hey!" Alan shouted to the crewman while waving his arm wildly. "Get outta there!"

From behind the vessel, in the shaft, an enormous mass of flesh a quarter the diameter of the shaft arose—clouds of insects partially obscuring it in a furious orbit. It rose, then settled, then rose higher. As more and more moved upward, the glossy, red, fleshy texture gave way to enormous crusted scales, then sickly white pulsing nodules that entirely covered the skin of the hideous creature. More tentacles snaked upward alongside the monster, searching for something to latch on to.

Alan stood frozen in shock.

The beast trumpeted a set of wails as it rotated to reveal a cluster of yellowed eyes that focused on the ships, its tentacles convulsing and gyrating wildly. Another tentacle found the landing limb and wrapped itself, changing color briefly in shocks of blue.

Suddenly, a blast, and a column of plasma flashed through the swarm of insects and singed the skin of the jungle beast. Another blast cleared a column of insects but did not quite reach the body.

Alan twisted around and saw Tier and Zu taking aim with their rifles from a perch above the landing limb. The other crewmen were shooting wildly with their pistols.

Alan turned back to the ships and saw Mup reaching Zu's vessel, struggling to maintain his footing while swatting at bugs of all sizes that clouded around the craft.

Alan slung the rifle over his back and charged toward Mup, keeping low. Still, bugs began pelting his jacket and face, and Alan couldn't help but reflexively swat at them. The buzzing and whirring were tremendous as Alan leapt into the small cargo bay.

"He's caught!" Mup exclaimed as he yanked at crates that had tumbled and locked up. The crewman pushed on the crates but grimaced, betraying that his legs were painfully caught.

A pair of rifle blasts from outside flared overhead, followed by a mighty trumpet from the beast and the tremendous shaking of the ship. Alan and Mup were flung to the opposite side of the cargo bay, Alan landing awkwardly against the rifle. He stumbled to his feet.

"That bastard is huge!" Mup yelled as he got back to pulling on the crates while flailing at bugs swirling within the bay.

The crewman yelped in pain and slapped at the crates pushing against him. "The mag-loader is jamming the crates against my legs! The mag-loader! The mag-loader!"

Alan slid next to Mup, and they desperately tried to make sense of the pile. Alan looked up and saw that the crewman's skin was spotted with winged insects, many crawling but others feeding.

"The mag-loader is behind me, and it's pulling the crates in! I'm caught!"

Mup and Alan scrambled to get behind the crewman, but the magnetic loader was pushed up against the bulkhead, with the crewman sandwiched between it and the crates it was pulling in piles over each other to get to the loader.

"I can't get to the shutoff!" Mup called as he waved bugs away from his ears.

Alan pushed his face close to the bulkhead so he could see along the wall and get a better view of the mag-loader's controls.

A heavy, resonating buzz filled the cargo bay, and the crewman screamed. Mup and Alan both looked up and found a bulbous insect larger than a human head wrapping its spindly legs around the man's face. Mup produced his pistol and shot the creature from the side, leaving a smoking hole in the bug's round abdomen spurting yellow slime. The crewman, covered in insect guts, used his free arms to throw the writhing carcass to the ground.

More rifle blasts sounded from outside and another quaking of the limb shook the vessel.

Mup returned to making sense of the loader.

Putting a hand on Mup's shoulder, Alan shouted, "See what you can do. I'll be right back!"

Alan ran out of the cargo bay, his boots crunching over the carcasses of bugs large and small. He turned and ran to the other ship, shielding his head with an arm. He reached the open door to the university ship and leapt in. *Bugs in here too!*

He flung luggage that had fallen onto a low chest, then flipped open the box. It was full of tools, once organized and now a mess. Alan briefly wondered if it was always kept this messy or if it was because of the violent shaking.

Spanner. Lamp. Hand saw. Nails.

Crowbar. *Perfect.*

Alan reached into the pile of tools and produced the bar. He quickly looked around the cockpit for anything else that would help. The camp pack.

He grabbed the yellow camp pack and slung it over his free shoulder. It was a bulky and awkward but vital if they had to camp on the planet.

He moved to the door and peeked out, quickly shaking his head to throw off a bug that had gotten tangled in his hair. He looked toward the jungle wall, then back toward the shaft, where he saw the angry monster and its swarm of insects still writhing wildly. The monster had a set of large burn wounds above its cluster of eyes, a mix of blue and yellow liquid pulsing out in rhythmic squirts.

Alan realized he was within a yard or two of the tentacle that had wrapped itself around the ships and the landing limb. He hadn't fully appreciated the amount of thick, wet spines and fine needles that covered the tentacle like a thin fur coat. *Don't want that thing to touch me.*

He leapt down from the ship and jogged backward, awkwardly fumbling to retrieve his rifle. Realizing it was too heavy to hold with one arm, Alan backstepped until he felt safely distanced, then went to one knee and put the bar at his side to free his other arm. He mentally noted he was close to the edge of the limb; if he began a slide, he would not recover and would fall into the abyss. He shouldered the rifle and looked down the sights, bringing the tentacle into alignment. He held his breath —

The rifle sizzled with heat, and where an invisible beam met the tentacle came a brilliant flare of silver light and a splitting crack of an explosion.

The tentacle split in two, both sides releasing their tension and flailing wildly — as if each controlled by an individual brain. The landing limb lurched up, bouncing both ships.

Alan's ship landed with a slight skid that quickly devolved into an uncontrolled slide, and over the side of the limb it continued. The vessel tipped and disappeared into the abyss, sending off a cloud of insects that abandoned it in its final descent.

The afterimage of the blast kept Alan partially blind in the center of his vision, but it was unmistakable what had just happened. He lowered the rifle in shock.

The other half of the tentacle began swinging through the air and knocked into the remaining ship. Alan saw Mup slip and fall inside the cargo bay.

Alan reached down to grab the crowbar but found only the surface of the limb. He looked to each side, then awkwardly turned to look over his back. The bar had slid into a teetering position near the drop-off.

Alan put the rifle down and threw the yellow backpack on top of it. He lowered himself onto his stomach and crawled slowly toward the bar. He sensed the slope of the limb's surface increasing, the sensation of gravity goading his body to start sliding into the abyss. *Almost... almost...*

He reached out and felt the touch of the bar just at his fingertips. The monster roared, its ugly moan echoing up the shaft over the sounds of its buzzing cloud of insects. Alan could sense the tentacle striking the limb, everything shifting beneath him, the bar moving just a little more out of his grasp.

He scooted forward, reaching...

A pair of hands grabbed his ankles tightly but didn't pull. Alan felt the balance they gave him, and without hesitation, he scooted forward just enough to firmly grasp the bar.

The hands began pulling steadily, and Alan moved back up the limb to safety. He rolled onto his back and found Tier kneeling over him, offering an arm dotted with crawling bugs.

"Thanks," Alan said as Tier lifted him to his feet. Tier grabbed the yellow backpack and rifle, then ran to the ship, with Alan following.

The two climbed into the cargo bay. Another wild tentacle slammed into the vessel, this time spinning the ship ninety degrees and sending Tier and Alan tumbling around the bay. The vessel had rotated, and now the creature's eyes were peering in at the group in the back of the cargo bay.

Alan leapt over debris and rushed to the forward bulkhead, where Mup struggled to reach the controls to the mag-loader. "Get this in there," Alan called, tossing the bar to Mup, "and yank the hook over the controls."

Tier steadied himself and quickly scanned the cargo bay. He moved to a pile of loose netting and pitched it to the back, uncovering a small crate marked with a slash of blue tape. He grabbed it with one hand and carried it toward the door of the cargo bay.

Tier turned his attention to the monster, its mosaic of alien eyes wildly scanning every direction. He did not see intelligence in the eyes, just a crazed animal driven by primitive reactions to stimuli.

He raised his rifle and took aim but held his shot, waiting for a break in the swarming insects.

The creature's tentacle again found the landing limb and reflexively hurled itself over the ship, around the limb, and back. It tightened, shifting the vessel and pulling the landing limb down enough to unbalance Tier for a moment.

Mup wedged the lever bar between the bulkhead and mag-loader. He pulled back on the lever to move the mag-loader away from the bulkhead, but it only resulted in a pained yelp from the stuck man. Mup released pressure and wedged the bar deeper behind the mag-loader until he could feel the hooked end pass beyond the control panel. He pulled the bar back to bring the hook in contact with the control panel and began vigorously shaking the bar to try to disengage the magnetic controls on the mag-loader.

Tier, back in sight over the creature's eye cluster, held his breath.

The loader chirped twice, and the crates fell from the man, no longer pulled in by powerful electromagnets.

"Grab him! Grab him!" Mup shouted.

Alan pulled at a crate, and it fell freely with Alan's efforts. He quickly cleared the pile to reveal the broken legs of the crewman. With a single effort, Alan rolled the man over his shoulders and stood.

Mup was already ahead of Alan, shoving a crate to the side to clear a path. Alan looked up and was shocked to see the vessel had oriented toward the creature.

Tier saw his clearing and fired the rifle; nearly instantly, another rifle also fired from the trees. The creature's eye cluster transformed into a brilliant nova of silver light and exploded. Carapace, burning flesh, and fluid soared dramatically through the air, raining into the jungle trees and all over the ship. The creature's body now had, where the eyes once were, a tremendous gaping hole all the way through, flesh hanging from the wound like a blooming flower.

Insects quickly swarmed over the fresh wound, covering it until it became a seething black mass.

The monster lurched to one side, fell dramatically, and paused.

Oh, no, Tier thought.

Then it fell again, this time falling farther before jerking to a stop. The landing limb heaved, and Tier instinctively grabbed hold of the ceiling net.

The creature slumped to the other side and fell, disappearing below the landing limb.

Across the shaft, Tier saw the creature's tentacles, already tense, begin shearing off the branches and limbs they were attached to.

Tier turned his head and saw the arm that was wrapped around the landing limb tense and yank, shaking the limb and cracking its interior.

"Run!" Tier shouted. *"Run!"* He threw his rifle over his shoulder, grabbed the cargo crate in his arms, and leapt out of the bay, running as fast as his feet could carry him.

Alan stumbled out of the cargo bay, trying not to let the load on his shoulders lead him into a fall into the abyss. Mup grabbed Alan's arm tightly and guided him to round the ship toward the jungle wall.

Alan ran as fast as he could while carrying the crewmember. As they passed underneath the tentacle gripping the landing limb, it tensed and crushed inward, slashing the group with its spines.

Alan sensed his head had been gashed, but he continued running with every ounce of vigor he could summon.

Mup and Tier ran ahead and reached the jungle wall. Tier threw the crate, backpack, and rifle into the jungle, then matched Mup in grabbing a thick vine and turning to extend an arm to Alan.

The tentacle seized a final time and yanked downward with tremendous force as the full weight of the creature's body came to bear. The landing limb snapped loudly, and an explosion of splintered wood shot into the air in front of Alan. An enormous crevice ripped through the limb where it met the jungle wall.

Alan used his momentum to hurl the crewman over his head, the man going farther than Alan had hoped. The man landed sideways in a cluster of tree branches, and he quickly entangled himself securely in vines.

The landing limb tilted down toward the abyss, Zu's ship sliding away and falling off silently.

With a final burst of effort, Alan sprinted up the increasing slope of the falling limb and leapt to the jungle wall as he reached the end of the branch. He glided gracefully through the air, then fell hard against the jagged break where the landing limb had once been attached. His torso fell over the top, his hips and legs dangling. Instinctively his hand reached out for anything to grip. Smooth wood and moss. He felt himself slipping and looked up just in time to see Mup and Tier arrive to his rescue, each reaching down and grabbing his arms.

They pulled him over the edge and Alan, now safe, rolled onto his back and threw an arm over his bloodied face. His chest rising and falling deeply, Alan lay staring up into the canopy.

"Unbelievable," he whispered between breaths. "Totally unbelievable."

Mup leaned over Alan. "Teamwork, right?"

Chapter 6
Regroup

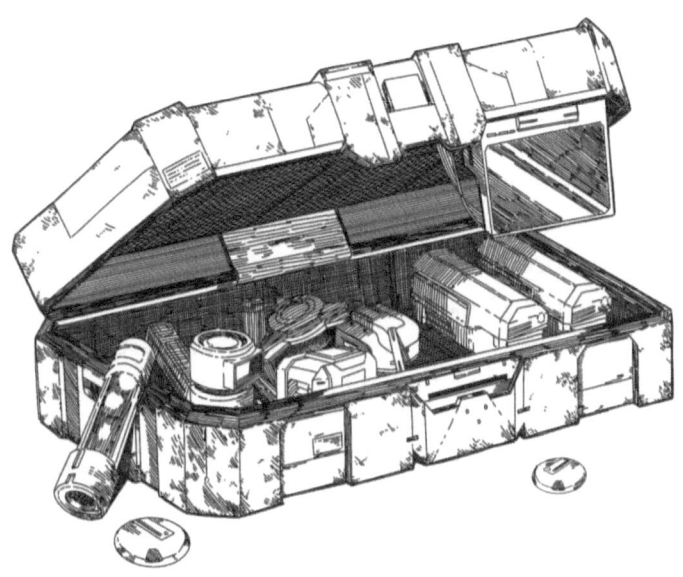

The warbling songs of birds and a constant symphony of insect drones had returned to the jungle.

From a perilous perch jutting over the jungle pit, Tier and Mup surveyed the depths of the abyss. The creature, when it died, had torn a tremendous amount of foliage from the trees that formed the shaft walls. Slashes of cleared limbs left the interior of the jungle exposed to sunlight and observation. Torn foliage, wrapped in the beast's arms, had fallen down the pit but gotten tangled and arrested the creature's fall. A few hundred feet below, the splayed creature had come to rest with its arms ensnared in the jungle trees on all sides of the pit and its gargantuan body limp and hanging as if in a hammock. Carrion eaters of all varieties had descended from the sky or appeared from the forest to feast on the monster, whose body had drained of fluid and turned its skin a mottle of gray. A mass of creatures fought through swarms of bugs for access to the wounded bits. With flesh obtained, the creatures scurried or flew off to a less contested spot on the corpse to eat their hard-won prize.

Neither of the ships could be seen. They had simply fallen past the monster into the darkness.

"It looks like we're here to stay," Mup quipped as he scanned the darkness with a monocular.

"Here to die," Tier replied.

Mup scanned the creature. He watched a group of furless green monkeys hiss and howl at each other, fighting for a spot near a blistered, oily wound.

"I hope there aren't more of those things down there," Mup said. "That beast was hideous."

"I've seen worse. On my home, we have beasts from the sea that make *that* look tame," Tier replied coolly. "When I was younger, I joined other boys to hunt *Zigwrat*. Giant beasts. Giant, destructive creatures. But we did not hunt sick ones. Not sick ones like that. What we did to *that*," —he flipped a hand toward the rotting creature —"was merciful."

Mup put down the monocular and looked to Tier. "What makes you think it was sick?"

"He was *wild* with sickness," Tier exhorted. "His eyes were hysterical, and he couldn't control his arms. Those insects that surrounded him and swarmed him — their eggs were in his skin. They were eating him alive, outside and inside, slowly... and he couldn't get away."

Mup sat shocked. "You are making me feel bad for the— filth squid." He looked down at the mess of flesh.

"For him, it was good we met."

Tier stood and carefully climbed away.

* * *

From a nearby nest of leaves and vines, Zu dug through the contents of one of the crates that had been saved before the landing limb snapped away into the abyss. Alan squatted next to another crate with an open lid and inspected the contents for anything useful to salvage.

Inside, neat gray boxes of electronics were stacked carefully. Alan lifted each box out gently and looked it over before reaching to the next box in the stack.

Compact ground radar, portable spectro, a trio of survey drones... this crate must be worth a fortune, Alan thought to himself. He pulled one of the drones from the neat pile on his left and put it on the right. *This is all military grade. He must have incredible funding.*

Alan recalled the contents of his own yellow camp pack: a fabric shelter, some light sleep coverings, a med kit, and two days of calories for two adults.

I need to stay close to Zu, Alan admitted to himself. *No margin for error. If we get injured, lost... Better to stick with the others.*

Alan placed the equipment of no immediate use back into the crate and closed the top. He swiped a finger across the front bezel of the lid, and the crate locked and sealed itself, flashing the lip of the crate green to confirm.

Drone in hand, Alan got up and walked to where Zu was placing items into a hiking pack. "Survey drone. You had a few, but we might only need one."

Zu opened the pack wide and angled it toward Alan. The sack was neatly stuffed with electronics boxes, silver pouches, and some tightly rolled fabric. He dropped the drone in.

Alan turned and surveyed the bramble.

The injured crewman was lying in a half-seated position in the crotch of a branch, one of his injured legs hanging. A second partner crewman had wrapped the broken leg in a textured fabric and was spraying a bottle of aerosol onto the wrap—hardening it. The injured crewman looked pale and, like everyone, was covered in a sheen of sweat.

The third crewman was on his knees, sorting through the second of two crates. He made a small pile of silver pouches but rejected whatever other contents were inside the crate.

A much smaller crate lay unattended in a nook under a branch. The size of a small backpack, the gray hard-shelled crate was marked with a slash of blue tape. Alan walked over to it and pulled it out from under the branch.

"No!" the crewman sorting the other crates shouted. "Leave that one alone. I already sorted it."

"Sorry, I didn't..."

"It is fine. Please." The crew member gestured to move away from the crate.

"My guides are a secretive bunch," Zu remarked with a smile over his shoulder. "Even from me. But they have always been good in a bind."

Zu finished his inspection and sealed the backpack securely with a tight roll. He stood, hoisted the pack up, and hung it on a branch with another pack and Alan's. He returned to the crate and locked it.

"Hope you don't mind sleeping under the stars," Zu remarked to the crew members.

Tier clambered down, swinging carefully from branch to branch, keeping a cautious hand on a vine when he arrived with the group.

"Karjan, *that's* what's useful?" he asked, looking at the packs.

The crewmember responded, "It's enough for a few days, if we ration and don't need shelter."

"But the best news is, we have the beacon," Zu assured.

Tier looked at Zu. "We'll need to be on top of the canopy to get the beacon signal up to an orbiting ship. This means a climb."

Karjan interjected, "If we climb to the canopy, we can't bring Rell. He can't walk. And the beacon — what good is it? There is no ship nearby — "

"It's the only chance," Tier interrupted. He thought briefly and continued, "Friend, it's a small chance, but we would be foolish not to try it."

"What of Rell?"

Rell spoke from his branch. "I will stay here. I can't burden you."

Tier looked at Rell's attendant. "You will stay here with him. We will leave you with what you need. When we get a signal, we'll send the rescuers down here and pick you up as well."

For a moment, a pregnant silence lingered over the conversation before Alan interjected, "I look forward to an ocean view."

Zu thought for a moment before he realized Alan was referring to the sibling planet. He ignored the comment as he turned to address Tier. "You will lead us to the canopy, then."

"Their guide will lead," Tier replied. "He knows the way — he's been here before."

Zu struggled to maintain a smile. "Then, their guide — "

"Mup," Alan interjected.

"Mup will lead. Very good."

Mup appeared from the shaft edge and found all eyes on him. He threw a thumb over his shoulder. "That thing is *dead*. Dead. Dead. Dead. We should get moving before it stinks up the jungle like a sick pig. Who's leading?"

Chapter 7
Climb

The group climbed slowly through the dense jungle forest. In the understory where the light infrequently reached, they moved over mostly bare branches and green vines. The ascent went quickly when a conveniently wide limb appeared that allowed them to walk for some distance before returning to climbing.

In all directions, the jungle appeared a chaotic mess of foliage and tree limbs. Frequently, an errant branch would snag a piece of clothing, or a pack, and had to be broken off.

Vines, ever-present and needing to be moved or cut, draped across walking limbs and branch tangles.

The occasional beam of light penetrated from above before landing on a broad-leaved water cupper or wide walking limb. Birds moved through the forest in short flights, from bramble to bramble, stopping to observe the group before moving on. All around, the chorus of animal cries continued.

Mup had climbed through the forest to the canopy before, when he had initially surveyed the planet. On his first trip, he had slowly and painstakingly discovered a winding path deep into the jungle that led up the fifteen-hundred-foot climb to the canopy. He had marked the path intermittently with slashes of red to find his way. In the three dimensions of the jungle understory, his tablet couldn't track his path and could provide little assistance — so he resorted to some of the most primitive skills of the explorer.

In the number of weeks since Mup had originally been on the planet and marked the path, the jungle had worked to erase his marks — either washing them to a light outline or hiding them with new growth. Mup led, using his memories and intuition, but continued the search for his marks. When they had gone far without coming across a red slash, he would backtrack until he could find the path.

Mup climbed the larger branches as they rose up and down in their random growth habits. Sometimes the limbs they walked upon moved horizontally through the jungle, but many times, they would slope up so steeply the group would have to jump to a nearby tangle of branches and climb slowly to where the branch leveled out again. The group moved cautiously, passing their crates and packs to each other as they moved across dangerous gaps in the path.

Tier kept the rear of the slow-moving group of travelers, always keeping an eye on where they had passed through. The constant cacophony of birdcalls and insect flutters made it difficult to detect stalkers. Pausing to watch for movement was of no great help either — the jungle was always moving, and the storm he sensed overhead did not help.

The rest of the group also sensed the darkness of cloud cover, even from the relative darkness of the jungle understory. The usual sounds of the jungle received a new addition: the sound of small water columns falling from above.

As the rain from the storm hit the canopy, the water coalesced onto leaves and pooled. When the weight was too much, the leaves would bend and pour their contents into the jungle below, where the action would repeat, aggregating into more and more vertical streams.

Mup watched as water fell in columns either a hundred feet tall or as small streams that wound down around vines. Everywhere, water moved lower and lower through the layers of the jungle.

Alan appreciated the water as he walked underneath unavoidable trickles from above. It washed away dried blood from thorn pricks, the sweat from his hair, the grime from his clothes. But Alan realized the price was an intense cloud of warm, suffocating humidity — even greater than at the landing limb.

Silently working their way upward, the group plodded on — even slower as the limbs and vines became dangerously slick.

Zu sensed the water streams becoming stronger as the storm continued above, but he also began feeling stray raindrops. Perhaps they were arriving close to the canopy. The limbs above, the vines hanging, they had begun swaying in unison — moving left slowly, creaking, then right. He paused to feel the jungle move.

"We must be getting close," Zu said.

Mup observed the shaking ceiling of branches not far above them. "Sounds like it's nicer down here."

"The heat cannot be more insufferable," Alan complained. "I'll take the rain."

"Prefer the lab, Dr. Alan? I thought you relished the chance to get dirty," Zu chided as he pulled himself over a fallen log.

"I'll take the lab over being suffocated with a hot, wet towel," Alan moaned.

Mup led the group along a broad limb and noted more frequent branches thick with leaves.

"This limb we are on," Mup said, "it's the last one. Then the tricky part—the vertical climb I warned you about."

Alan mulled over whether he was happy to escape the understory or terrified to make a sustained climb in the rain.

After a few minutes, Alan saw ahead what looked like a natural wall—it went down as far as he could see and appeared to rise all the way to the canopy. Covering the wall was a puzzle of interlocking slabs of textured wood. The gradual curvature of the structure revealed its true identity—they had reached a tremendous tree trunk.

The trees of Helios were gargantuan but difficult to judge because they were hidden underneath an impenetrable canopy of leaves. Up close, Alan guessed the tree must be miles tall, because the trunk looked like a flat surface, the curve in its face so gentle as to be imperceptible.

"It's a dead tree," Mup called from ahead. "We climb it straight up. Jagged on top; used to be taller, but—" He mimed a falling tree with his arms. "It snapped and fell a while ago."

"How is the climb?" Alan shouted ahead.

"The climb? It's good—just don't fall," Mup replied.

The group arrived at the wall, and Alan inspected the surface of the trunk. Its bark, like the tree itself, was of a large proportion. The jigsaw puzzle of bark plates created dark channels that zigzagged all over the surface. Some channels were broad enough that Alan guessed he could fit his entire body inside it and rest, securely, if he wanted to. Water trickled down many of the grooves.

Alan slapped the tree. The bark was solid and rough like sandstone.

"The top isn't too far," Mup said to the group. "It'll take you twenty minutes."

"Have you made the climb with a pack?" Karjan asked, looking up the wall.

Mup followed Karjan's gaze. "Yeah. Just go slow and keep your body near the wall so your pack doesn't pull you off. If you get tired, just find one of the larger grooves, swing in, and rest. Straight up."

The group paused.

Mup acknowledged the hesitation. "One of you has to go first. I can only help from behind the climb."

Tier pulled the straps on his pack tight, then stepped up and grabbed a slab. He pulled at the wedge, firmed his grip, planted a boot into a channel, and began climbing.

Alan took a deep breath, tightened the straps on his pack and rifle, and stepped up to the wall. "Always up for a good climb," he said as he threw himself to the first handholds.

He had not felt nervous on the ascent through the jungle, even though it had been just as dangerous. Being on a vertical wall made him anxious, and he feared the others sensing his trepidation, so he focused on each hand making progress upward.

As he climbed, he found himself a few yards underneath Tier. Focusing on Tier's route and climbing work relieved Alan's stress. Climbing with another person nearby eased the sense of heightened danger.

A few minutes in, Alan's pace had slowed down. Tier moved steadily upward, and Alan feared losing his partner. He considered calling out for Tier to pause, but he thought otherwise and looked for a channel to rest in.

Alan leaned back to survey the trunk, then quickly realized his error as the pack pulled heavily at him away from the wall. He hauled his chest back against the tree. Cautiously, he leaned his head back and spied the largest crevice he could reach. Heavy droplets of water falling parallel to the trunk spattered against his face. He quickly wiped the water out of his eyes with a hand and continued climbing toward a large break he had seen in the bark.

The break was indeed a crevice large enough to accommodate him completely. He moved in, realizing the climb out might be difficult, and rolled the pack off his back and settled it next to him. The shape of the crevice formed a natural seat, the neighboring bark plates forming the walls and ceiling of the small resting spot.

Alan stretched his back and shoulders — the weight of the pack now gone. He extended his fingers repeatedly and massaged both of his forearms. He realized he had been out of breath as he now caught it.

The world outside the resting spot was green and wet. They were within the canopy. Branches were obscured by an ever-present carpet of flat, waxy leaves, themselves covered in beads of water.

Alan had been in the snowy city of Denarii for years. He had forgotten the pleasures of lush nature without having ever realized it. No buildings. No colored lights and shrill holo-ads. No people. Just animals, trees, and rain.

As he watched the jungle and listened to the rain, a green monkey appeared, dropping from the canopy above onto a branch outside his hideaway. The monkey clung to the branch, which bounced lazily with the animal's arrival. The monkey looked to the jungle, then to the canopy before it turned its head to reveal its dinner-plate-sized yellow eyes.

Alan and the creature's gaze met, and the monkey froze.

His pulse jumped as he realized he was vulnerable to the wild animal, but as he looked into the monkey's eyes, he recognized no hostility. In the creature's face, he saw a mirrored curiosity.

The monkey moved slightly to make a comfortable perch of the branch, never taking its eyes off Alan. The two sat in a stare.

Without warning, the monkey turned its body to leap away, hesitated with a backward glance at Alan, then disappeared into the jungle.

I have been missing this, he thought. *It's been too long.*

Alan emerged above the canopy and crested the trunk a short while later. He threw his pack down, collapsed into a squat, and threw his head back, eyes closed, to gulp the fresh air and feel the light drops of rain fall against his body. Around him, he heard the others similarly recovering.

Satiated, he opened his eyes and stood up.

The top of the tree had been broken off many hundreds of years before. At the break was a cragged, pockmarked plateau of life growing from the dead trunk's remains. Across the landscape, strangler vines, brush flowers, cup leaves, and broad leaves decorated the sun-facing surface. Rotting wood and collected debris composted, forming the soil needed for plant life to spring up. Dark wooden pinnacles broke through the sea of green, keeping any space from being suitable for a ship to land, and looming over the terrain like ominous monoliths.

The pillars that dotted the landscape were sometimes man-sized and other times tall enough to cast shadows for great lengths. He realized it all must have gone on for nearly a mile, but he couldn't see through the forest of brush and wood shards.

The dead trunk of the tree was home to a unique ecosystem of plants that could not survive a few hundred feet below in the canopy's shade, let alone the thousands of feet to the dark surface of the planet. The mesa was an island in a sea.

Looking up, he gasped.

The storm clouds were broken, and behind them, the dark planet of Ceto loitered, covering half of the sky. He had never seen a planet so close without looking from the deck of a spacecraft. As he realized this, Alan felt the sensation of hanging by his feet, looking down at the surface of another planet.

The ocean of Ceto was plainly visible. It was a mostly clear day on the other planet, and he could see the spattering of islands that dotted its oceans. The islands were easy to recognize; they were tall, jagged mountains erupting from the ocean, a few of them covered in snow. With the planet as close as it was, he could vividly see the shadows cast by the mountain islands onto the ocean. As his gaze moved across the planet's surface, he could see the islands for whom the day was ending — their mountains illuminated in brilliant pink light and their shadows stretching for distances.

Alan realized the planet would eventually kill him and everything on the two worlds.

He turned his gaze from Ceto and took in the crater valley in which he stood. It was a magnificent sea of trees within a tremendous mountain-lined bowl, columns of light brilliantly illuminating far-off patches, while the rest slept under the shade of the passing storm.

Birds, undeterred by rain, swept along the surface of the canopy, moving freely at great speeds and distances.

Mup's voice appeared. "It's wonderful, but if you aren't careful, something will eat you."

"Thank you, Mup," Alan said, turning around.

Mup pointed up. "Keep an eye on the sky." He smiled. "Remember what I said when we flew in? Watch out for birds. You can still end up flying through a bird, just this time through their mouth."

Alan waited until Mup moved on to glance toward the sky. Wide-winged birds circled lazily far above.

* * *

The group found Mup's previous campsite. It was a shallow pit, cleared of plants, with a raised area still scorched from a campfire. Surrounding the pit was a jumble of wood splinters and natural spires, and the tangles of creeping vines. The structures of wood had been pitted and marred by the passage of time, some holes in the surface deep enough to provide shelter for a resting man.

"The beacon is transmitting," Karjan reported as he stood. A white globe sat quietly on a shelf at the top of an errant wood splinter. "It's got a good line of sight, nearly horizon to horizon," he said, looking over the broad crater. "If there's anyone out there, they'll hear it."

"You picked a good camp spot," Tier remarked as he unloaded the camping equipment from his pack.

"I like to think so," Mup replied. "You can store packs in some of these hideaways." Mup pointed to a set of the many hiding spots the interior of the tree trunk afforded.

Zu approached Mup. "Evening can't be too far off. You said you were last here to observe the natives, right?"

Mup glanced at Alan, then answered, "Yes."

"So, if you stayed here—" Zu motioned to the ground. "Then it's because the natives are nearby. Introduce us, won't you?"

Alan stepped in. "Yes, introduce us."

Zu continued, focused on Mup, "If there's a chance of a settlement, they will know…"

Mup replied, "There is certainly no settlement that will help us get off the planet. These are primitive natives. Don't be confused."

"Oh, I'm not confused. I've just found that in situations like this, it's best not to rule anything out."

"Zu is always an optimist," Alan said.

"Always," Zu repeated.

Mup paused, then relented. "Sure, just leave your stuff here… and he'll have to stay to watch our things." Mup pointed to Karjan, who shrugged. "Let's go meet the Heliops."

* * *

A ten-minute walk from the campsite, through the lush tropical landscape of the plateau, led to the edge of the trunk. Mup turned and followed the edge south. The group continued in silence, focusing on walking up, down, and through the various obstacles of plants and terrain.

The group moved slowly past a patch of plants that had obviously been tended, a garden among the jungle. Large, spiraling red stems rose from bases of thin-leaved bushes and arced five or six feet into the air above the trunk floor. Hanging from the towering stalks of the plant, yellow clusters of fruit clumped tightly together. Alan paused to take note, then continued.

As they moved along, an enormous bird with a wingspan ten times that of a man's arm span rose from behind a wooden pinnacle. The bird flapped three times with focused strength to rise fifty feet vertically, then brought in its wings toward its body, rolled onto its side, and dove out of sight over the edge of the trunk. The group watched expectantly and then caught sight of the creature, wings outstretched again, flying away over the canopy. A silhouette of a figure riding the back of the bird was plainly visible.

"That was a Heliop," Mup announced.

"The bird? I thought you said —" Zu asked.

"No, the Heliop was riding the bird. I don't know what to call the bird."

"Heliosteed?" Alan suggested.

"I don't know where they go on their 'Heliosteed', but I assume it's another village."

"Amazing!" Zu responded.

"They keep the birds in paddocks. You'll see." Mup continued the hike. "We're almost there."

As they moved forward, Tier kept his focus away from the edge of the tree trunk, toward the interior. He stopped. Mup, sensing Tier's alertness, also stopped.

Ahead of Tier's gaze, the sound of four shrill chitters emerged, but neither Mup nor Tier could see its source.

"Heliop," Tier said.

"Don't worry. They don't bite," Mup said to Tier. "Well, they bite. Just not us. Hopefully."

"Yes," Tier replied.

Chapter 8
Village

The group continued along a trail that appeared, and as they rounded a turn by a cluster of splintered monoliths, they got their first sight of the Heliop village nestled on the southern tip of the tree. The village had view with a wide panorama of the crater valley.

Alan at once made a visual census of the population of the small village — he quickly counted at least three groups of ten. The Heliops' appearance was not far off from Mup's succinct description: the creatures certainly resembled bipedal rodents slightly larger than a human child. Their fur had great diversity of color: blue, red, dark green, brown, and how they decorated their bodies was equally unique. While the creatures were tailless, all possessed expressive, large, round ears that rotated, twitched, and flattened in their conversations. On the tip of each of their long faces was a large nose.

The village itself was centered around a cluster of ten small, domed thatch shelters—a number with drifting smoke coming out of a hole at the apex. Around the shelters were work areas with tools and flat surfaces. To the side of the village was the Heliosteed paddock Mup had recalled—a series of large enclosures made of branches lashed into grids with vines. There were enclosures for at least fifteen Heliosteed, with many occupied by the large creatures.

A familiar set of four chitters split the air.

A few of the creatures quickly stood erect and looked to the visitors while the others froze in their seated positions. The sentry Heliops, sensing they were being observed, twitched their ears and turned their heads back and forth in a slow rhythm—the meaning lost to the men. After a moment, the seated Heliops rose and cautiously, with flat ears, began walking out of their work areas toward the group. Then, with a single long whistle from a sentry, the group lost any sense of hesitancy. Their ears perked, and they all rushed out to the men.

"They are friendly; don't freak out," Mup cautioned as the pack of thirty large rodents trotted out to the group.

Within a few seconds, Alan and the other men found themselves swarmed by the Heliops. The creatures did not fear physical contact with the visitors. The tribe tussled around the men, smelling the arms and hands of the group. Zu, Karjan, and Mup held their arms uncomfortably at shoulder height to avoid the intrusive creatures' noses in vain, while Tier stood still and tolerated the inspection. The smell of Heliop, dusty with a hint of fruit, filled the men's noses. Alan smiled widely and held his hands out to let the Heliops inspect them top to bottom.

As each creature took its turn to inspect a man, its ears were fully alert and erect and its nose working furiously to observe the strange smells. With inspection complete, each creature settled back into the crowd to coo and whistle among themselves in what Alan could only assume was a conversation about the new arrivals.

"All right. All right now," Zu called to a blue Heliop aggressively inspecting his elbow. "Mup, do you know how to communicate with them?"

"Do you know how to talk to a rat you just met?" Mup chided.

"You told us you stayed with them before."

"Yeah, to set up cameras and record them, not to become a member of the tribe," Mup said.

"Can — you — understand — me?" Zu said slowly, with no effect on the Heliops. "Can — you — understand — me?"

"They can't understand you," Mup interjected.

"I can see that, Mup, thank you," Zu replied, slightly irritated. "Tier, hand out the gifts."

Tier unfroze and pulled out a handful of screws and bolts from a pocket hidden on the inside of his pants. He held out the pile cautiously but purposefully. A brave, green-furred Heliop took one of the bolts and quickly twirled it with his small, clawed fingers. The creature sank back into the crowd, and others replaced it, each taking one of the silver objects from Tier's hand.

Alan saw the creatures did not appear excited about the gifts but did not give them up either.

The Heliops at the edges of the crowd, the ones that had already inspected the visitors and received their small gift, withdrew back to their work areas. They sauntered away slowly, trading among themselves.

Soon, the last of the Heliops was walking back to the village.

"That's it?" Karjan asked, arms finally lowered.

"We go interview some and see if we can find out about any other settlements that might have ships," Zu replied with a smile to Alan.

Mup and Alan exchanged glances.

The group walked to the Heliop village. As they arrived within the boundaries of the work areas, Zu approached various Heliops and, catching their attention, began miming signs that confused even Alan. The Heliops quickly became uninterested in Zu's miming interrogations and began walking away if he selected them.

While Zu moved from Heliop to Heliop, Alan saw what the creatures were working on diligently: leather craft. Piles of pre-cut leather were being shaped and decorated. They were creating long braids of leather rope, bags with belts and... saddles. *Ah, they are making saddles and bridles for the Heliosteed. A lot of flourishes and effort beyond what is needed.* He moved to the next group and saw that they were working with the material in its earlier form; they were cutting and shaping the leather hide with what looked like—

A knife shaped in blue and red metal.

Seed metal. No doubt about it. Just like Mup said.

Alan, realizing that Seed metal was in the village, searched for more. It was, as Mup had recalled, everywhere when Alan knew to look for it. It adorned pierced ears, decorated the entrance to shelter. Seed metal was all over.

Alan saw that some of the Heliops had begun glancing at Zu over their shoulders with flat ears. Zu was moving through the groups, calling attention to his hand signals.

"Zu," Alan called, "I think you are annoying them."

"Feel free to help," Zu shot back with reproach in his voice.

"I will, but I don't think they are open right now," Alan replied.

Zu cornered a Heliop. "Ship. Fly. Far." He spoke while miming with his hands.

"Zu, I'll stay for a bit. You go back to the camp and use the survey drone," Alan offered.

Alan read Zu's reaction—the Heliops would not be the breakthrough needed to escape the planet. The drone was the next-best possibility.

The cornered Heliop slipped away.

"Yes, clever idea," Zu replied. "See if you can get them to tell you about—"

"A settlement with a ship," Alan finished.

"Yes. Exactly."

"See you at the camp in a bit." Alan patted Zu on the shoulder as he passed. Tier followed.

"Mup." Alan grabbed Mup's arm and waited for Tier and Zu to get out of earshot. "You were right."

"That there are no ships and the Heliops don't like Zu?"

"No. Well, yes about the ships." Alan paused, letting go of Mup. "But you also never mentioned the Heliops not liking Zu."

"But they don't."

"Right. But the point we care about—you were right about the Seed artifacts. They are everywhere."

Mup looked around. "They are. I said they would be."

"And you were right," Alan continued. "Here is the plan: you go back with Zu and Tier and see if there is anything you can do to get us off this planet, and I'll..." Alan paused. "I'm good at this kind of thing—talking to locals."

"You don't speak their language," Mup interrupted.

"But I'm good at learning—"

"You can't chitter."

"Mup, listen to me. I'm a professional anthropologist. That's why you came to me with the Seed artifact and not to a chef."

"That doesn't even—"

"Mup, I am good at first-contact communications," Alan said, satisfied to have found what he wanted to say. "You go help Zu and Tier, and I'll stay and figure out something with the Heliops. Trust me."

Mup thought about it, then admitted quietly, "Alan, I don't think we're going to get off this planet."

Alan looked at the Heliops, the whole village furiously working leather from hides into saddles.

"Mup, you are probably right," Alan conceded. "But if we do, it'll be a great story."

* * *

Alan walked through the village. The creatures were wonderfully comfortable with strangers; they ignored Alan as he moved about. He peeked his head into the entrances of the shelters but did not dare to enter at the risk of turning the Heliops' favor as Zu had. As he peeked in the first shelter, he was surprised to discover the shelter floor was dug out to give the interior more vertical space than would be assumed from the outside. The resultant structure was larger than otherwise would have been possible.

As he surveyed the village, Alan realized that something was missing: the children. There were no children in the village.

Alan passed behind the village and looked over the wide panorama. The Heliops had chosen the location for its unobstructed morning-to-evening sunlight—or so Alan assumed. He extended his arm and measured the fist-widths between the sun and the horizon: three. He still had a little time to explore before dark.

He turned and headed past the paddocks. The large birds—beasts—stirred in their enclosures.

The Heliosteed were tremendous creatures with feather colors and patterns as unique as the Heliops. Each full, stocky body was juxtaposed by a craning neck upon which their long, slender head rested. A long spear of a beak led to the face of the bird, with a set of fist-sized eyes and, at the crest of the head, a swept-back plume of feathers. The talons of the birds were covered by a set of leather skirts, but as the creatures shuffled in their paddocks, the tapping of the claws on the hard wooden ground revealed the creatures' latent ability to deal great harm.

Each bird kept a piercing red eye on Alan as he walked by. None made a noise, but each turned to track his movements.

Alan made his way to the trail that led into the village. He followed it back out until he reached the garden of tall fruit plants. He paused, took a breath, and made a long whistle— his best impression of the Heliops' sentry whistle he had heard in the village.

From among the fruit plants erupted a chorus of high-pitched chitters and rustled leaves. He sat down casually, facing the plants. With another breath, he whistled, this time in the form of a song.

Tiny Heliop heads appeared among the fruit plants. *Children.*

The children moved toward Alan, their ears fluttering between flat and full as they approached. Putting his hands to his ears, Alan mimed full ears and smiled.

The Heliop children whistled and chittered and came rushing forward with full ears. *Laughing at how dumb I look.*

From the plants appeared twenty Heliop youth, nearly all golden yellow in color. Like the adults, they swarmed around him and pressed their noses into his clothing, gently using their hands to manipulate Alan's arms. From his seated position, the youth were slightly taller and could move their noses through his hair. He instinctively swatted a nose that sniffed into his ear and laughed. The youth chittered in response in their form of laughter.

Alan locked eyes with a Heliop standing in front of him. Alan pointed to himself and moved his hand in a waving motion. The Heliop blinked and listened, its ear steady and alert. Alan repeated the hand gesture while pointing to himself. With exaggeration, Alan jabbed his chest and waited for the creature. It hesitated, so he repeated the jab, and the Heliop held up its hand and motioned a wave that repeated Alan's sign. Alan smiled, and the crowd exploded in coos and whistles.

The youth were delighted to interact with Alan, and each competed to have a turn at creating a sign to use with Alan.

A gyrating hand toward the sky indicated the nearby fruit plants. A pulsing fist, the ground. Alan had introduced two hands together with waving fingers as a bird. A waving fist, the looming planet of Ceto. A brief passing rain led to a Heliop child suggesting a descending hand with waving fingers as rain, which Alan repeated.

With some difficulty, they established a fist with a protruding thumb sideways as singular Heliop and the thumb upwards as the aggregate of Heliops. It had taken some of Alan's learned tricks to determine whether the thumb and fist was an individual Heliop's name or the species as a whole.

Alan signed to the enthralled audience: Man. Walk. Question.

A few of the youth understood quickly, pointed along the path that they were sitting on, and then pointed down the path toward Alan's camp. One youth held up three fingers, then again pointed toward the camp.

Good. Now a hard one.

Alan signed: Man. More. Question.

Not having a sign for *anywhere*, Alan mimed looking all around.

The Heliops looked at each other and chittered among themselves, ears quivering. They came to a consensus, and the Heliop closest to Alan signed: No. Question.

Okay. Maybe they don't understand.

Heliop. More. Question.

The youth immediately pointed toward the village.

Satisfied, Alan mimed: Heliop. More. Question.

The youth paused, then stood, looked to the horizon, and pointed strongly in five different directions, then returned to a squat.

The other Heliop villages. Now that we have primed the conversation...

Alan repeated the original query: Man. More. Question.

This time, the Heliop stood, pointed to the camp, then returned to his squat and signed: Man. More. No.

Alan sighed and lowered his head. It was clear the Heliop understood the question. It was clear there were no other men on the planet.

Alan had been caught up in the hope for an escape — a simple way off the planet and a tale of getting by with the slimmest of margins. It would not happen. The cruel truth pressed against Alan. In a few days, he and everything around him would be returned to their original form of atoms floating through space.

Chapter 9
Fate

Evening had fallen on the jungle of Helios, and a perfectly clear sky set the stage for the duality of stars to the south and the setting profile of the nearby sister planet of Ceto to the north. The planet sank below the horizon, and with it, the light reflected from its oceans. The sky glowed a dull green as Ceto's light illuminated the evening from beyond the horizon.

The creatures of Helios retreated to their roosts as the nocturnal animals crept out to explore for the evening. The chorus of insects had changed tone; a constant buzz had been replaced by thousands of hollow clicks from all around. Alan walked along the edge of the tree and turned to follow the dancing light of a campfire.

Zu, Tier, Karjan, and Mup were at the camp. They had unpacked their sleep gear and were circled around the tidy campfire set on an elevated bowl of charred wood. Zu was changing to another shirt, and Tier worked his tangled hair into a cleaner mess. Mup sat on his ledge, staring into the fire. Karjan, the farthest from the fire, was working with equipment.

As Alan walked into camp, Karjan looked up from the survey drone he was folding back into its case. "Alan, we were starting to worry you had become someone's dinner." The others looked up from around the fire with a mix of surprise and relief.

Alan waved half-heartedly in response and walked over to the hole he had stuffed his sleeping equipment in.

"You must have learned something good," Mup said with a sense of cheer as he sat up. "You were gone for hours!"

"I was able to communicate with some of the Heliops, the cubs. That was certainly interesting. I would like to work with them more. They are smart, inventive, and picked up signing fast."

"Where is the nearest settlement?" Zu stood. "With a ship?"

Alan looked at Zu. "There is none. There are no human settlements here. Only other Heliop villages... all around."

"Are you sure? How can you be sure?"

"I'm certain. They were clear."

"But how can you be certain? Maybe they misunderstood — maybe it was a language barrier. Maybe it was — "

"I'm certain, Zu. I was there," Alan replied.

Zu looked into Alan's face for a sign of hope and found none. He sat back down. "Perhaps tomorrow you try again."

"Tomorrow. The Heliops are bright and eager to share. To be honest, I haven't seen an uncontacted group this open to outsiders. It's like we have been living near them for years."

Silence surrounded the campfire.

No one is mentioning the beacon. Or the surveyor. Need not bring it up, Alan thought.

Alan pulled out his equipment with a jerk and released the sleeping bag. He rolled it out over his section of flat campground and struggled to settle it into place.

Karjan locked the drone case and walked back to his bedding with the box, packed it away in a rotted nook, then squatted down to sit on his sleeping roll. He looked into the small campfire: "We came to a trap."

In the far distance, in the jungle beyond the tree, an animal cried out, followed by a chorus of screeches — then all ambience was returned to the clicking songs of the night insects.

Mup spoke. "If the trap hadn't sprung, we would be competing to find the origin of the artifact. We would have been in different camps. Maybe we would have been here, and you would have been somewhere else."

"I guess that's true," Zu responded with a slight tone of regret. "It's a shame. I'll admit I was very excited by the possibilities of this planet. Very excited. In the lab, we have been working so long with the same tiny set of artifacts. The whole collection is so small you could fit them in your shoe. If there is more of what you found, Mup… a whole world…" Zu trailed off in thought.

After a moment, Zu spoke again, his tone pleasant. "Alan, you won't believe what I left in order to come here and be trapped on this planet with you."

Mup lay on his side toward the group as Alan sat on his own bedding and faced the fire. "I'm sure you can't wait to tell me."

"One of our scouts, he was sent off to do a ground survey on... on..."

"Beta Ceti Minor."

"Beta Ceti Minor. Thank you, Tier." Zu smiled. "He was sent off to do a ground survey and prepare a landing zone for some researchers — but he didn't check in after he landed. Beta Ceti Minor is a cold rock planet. It's got a good atmosphere — but it's a perpetual snowstorm. A lot of things could have happened — most likely he got lost in a whiteout. But he's an experienced scout, and there was a good chance he could survive in the conditions, so they sent a search party. The search party lands, finds his ship easily, and asks the ship, 'Where is he?' The ship points to its last record of him, and the party goes to it. It leads them right to a cave — a cave with an airlock deep inside."

Alan rubbed his chin and listened as Zu continued.

"The search party goes inside the airlock and finds an advanced facility — atmosphere controlled, powered, automated — and totally dark. They begin exploring — and they encounter... you won't believe it..."

"Okay, tell me," Alan said.

"They find a civilization of sentient robots, abandoned for thousands of years. They had abducted the scout when he stumbled upon them... and kept him in a menagerie within the facility. A menagerie of other creatures that had either lived on the planet before it iced over —"

"Or creatures that were unlucky enough to stumble across the zookeepers," Alan finished.

"Exactly. But *unlucky* is a curious choice of words. The *zookeepers*, as you call them, took particularly loving care of their stock. Our scout was found in a tremendous underground cavern, artificial, that was created to mimic a perfect planet—from our perspective. A world of dreams. An artificial ecosystem with sunlight, green trees, clean water, gentle breeze, wild creatures, game, fruit. Everything you would need to keep your residents happy—for generations." Zu smiled, his eyes bright. "And there *were* residents who had been there for many generations. So many generations, they didn't know when it began. When we rescued our man, the others in the zoo didn't want to go. It was all they had known."

"How did the rescuers not end up in the zoo?" Mup asked.

"I didn't hesitate to make examples," Tier replied.

Mup raised an eyebrow.

"Tier was a little more aggressive than I would have preferred, but that's why he carries the weapons," Zu said.

"And the zookeepers let you escape with the scout?" Alan asked.

"We didn't have to escape. As soon as Tier demonstrated we could defend ourselves, they rolled back to a program that was amicable to visitors."

Alan leaned forward. "And you could study them."

"Exactly. We brought the destroyed Ceti-bot back to the university lab on Denarii for study."

Alan smiled broadly. "I have so many questions."

"I knew you would. First contact—with a non-biologic civilization. It's exactly up your alley."

Alan realized it *was* exactly up his alley. His breakthrough contribution to Seed civilization research was pioneering techniques for making sense of alien computers, technology, and data formats. To interface with a robotic civilization…

"I don't get it," Mup interrupted, shaking his head. "Why haven't you been working together? Why do you both actively *avoid* working together? The sum of you two is greater than your parts."

Zu laughed and looked at Mup. "Alan and I have a bit of a philosophical disagreement, you could say."

Alan pointed at Mup. "A foundational disagreement."

"Who history belongs to?" Mup asked.

"Who the *past* belongs to," Zu corrected.

All the eyes in the camp fell upon Alan; he didn't need to look up from the fire to sense it. He stared into the fire, then looked up at Mup.

"History is not just an observation of the past, but how we interpret it," Alan said. "We carry it with us and are unconsciously controlled by it in many ways, and past is present in all we do."

Alan looked to Tier and continued, "Religion could be considered history—and it certainly impacts what we do. If you shed light on a truth and that discovered truth alters a civilization's orientation—its principal bedrock of beliefs…" He paused for a moment. "Old structures of culture and civilization could fall as if in a tremendous earthquake."

Karjan looked at Tier as Tier remained fixed on Alan.

"But ultimately," Alan resumed, "the truth has to be discovered and shared. It is the cleanest contract with our ancestors, ourselves, and those that will come after us. To be open and transparent with the truths that history reveals is not a right but a responsibility."

"What if a good society is based on a lie?" Tier asked Alan. "If the society is good—peaceful, fair, happy—then the lie is therefore good—and it must be preserved. If your mother was honest and raised you well—but in her youth committed a terrible act, what is the *virtue* in surfacing that truth despite a lifetime of repentance?"

"Judge the tree by the fruit..." Mup added softly.

Alan quietly contemplated Tier's position as Zu turned to Mup.

"History is a part of us, Mup," Zu said. "It is a part of who we are and how we make our choices—which is precisely why it must be placed under the conservatorship of those who are already entrusted to guide our civilization. History, how it is presented, how it is preserved, how it is archived, how it is discovered—these are all mechanisms of great leverage to bring societies together or to pull them apart. They are the most powerful levers, in fact—and they must be entrusted to the most powerful."

The entire group was quiet. The stars above had appeared, brighter than ever as Ceto's reflected light had all but disappeared far below the horizon.

Alan broke the silence and wondered aloud, "What if we somehow survive this? What if we survive this and discover the source of the artifact? Who will it belong to?"

Zu looked at Alan with a smile. "Let me say this: Alan, you are an incredible man."

Alan was shocked, but he steadied himself to not show it.

"I have heard some say you are an amateur because you work separately from the Core Alliance," Zu said. "Would you know that when you published that paper on bifurcating Seed artifact network channels with gamma... the guys in the lab, it moved them forward two years. You published it like an invitation to a party but never knew that thirty light-years away, a team of bright computer archaeologists were going over every sentence three times. It unlocked so much work.

Millions and millions in funding, only to be passed by an 'amateur.'

"Let me repeat. I have entire teams of research scientists back in my labs, the brightest I can find. And they have intelligence — loads of it. But they do not have what you have — wisdom. If I brought my guys, they'd be trying to get a computer to talk to the Heliops, making studies and observations, trying to reverse-engineer their cultural codes so that we could figure out that 'cheep' meant hello. But you, on the other hand, one look at the Heliops and you sensed how they operated, and you dove in. You looked at the entire picture. And now we know for certain that we're doomed to die here." Zu and the rest laughed. "But it's true. You have an incredible talent that is unique.

"And let me admit something to you here: I've been saddened by your disappearance from the field for the last few years. Imagine where we would have been if all this time we had been working together. My resources and your intellect. Only serves to wonder.

"When we don't come back — when they write about us, write our obituaries — mine will no doubt be longer and read by more people — "

"No doubt." Alan smiled dryly.

" — but yours will say more. They won't have to write it, but it will say it: 'Did far more with far less.' What does that say about me?"

Alan swallowed as silence fell on the group. He had never considered that Zu gave any thought to him or his work.

Zu continued, "If the price for working with you is working in the open, and if we survive this mess — we should work together. Amateurs."

Alan looked at Zu and nodded.

The fire's light danced on Tier's face as he spoke, "If we *do* find the source of the Seed, and it *does* reveal a truth about the origin of the universe, it could shake, *destroy*, the core of untold numbers of civilizations. Isn't that a price too high for a truth?"

Zu's gaze was lost in the campfire. "Maybe it's just the price we have to pay. Maybe our creation myths are a debt that got our civilizations to this point, and a truth like what the Seed civilization can show us about the origin of the galaxy… that is the payment coming due. We've owed it all along."

Mup watched quietly through the fire as Tier rapped his fingers together anxiously.

Chapter 10
Heliosteeds

In the morning, Alan woke to insects flying over his ears and mouth. He swatted at them, half awake, but sleep was irrecoverable.

The sky was a faint pink, halfway between night and day. Alan threw off his light sleeping cover; it had been cold in the evening, and a chill breeze had swept through in the deep of the night. The sleeping cover had not been enough, and Alan had spent the evening struggling to find a position that was both comfortable and warm. He sat up and saw that he was the first to rise. It was no longer bitterly cold, but it was not warm yet either.

My last sunrise? My last morning? Alan thought.

He sat, looked around, and, for a moment, wished it were a dream he could escape from. But it was not. As his body and brain woke, the certainty of reality settled in. Yet still, he felt a hollow sadness over his fate. His inner spirit still clung to the notion that there was a way out that had simply not been discovered yet. *Only one day to find out.*

He rose and stretched, swatted another bug, and began quietly putting on his shoes. Despite his polite attempts to be discrete, the others shifted in their beds. Mup rolled over, his eyes barely open.

The rest got up, slowly and silently. Alan heated water with the chemothermal cooker and prepared a morning soup from dried concentrate. He poured the thick soup into cups for each of the rising party and handed them out.

"I'm going back to study the Heliops," Alan announced.

Mup rubbed his eyes as he accepted Alan's soup. "I'd like to go. I'm curious about them."

"I'll go too," Zu said. "Karjan, Tier, will you continue the search patterns on the drone and attend the beacon?"

Tier nodded.

When breakfast was settled, Zu, Mup, and Alan settled on what to bring for the day trip: freeze-dried lunch, a light load of water, the emergency med pack, and a personal computer.

As they loaded the compact daypack, Mup handed Alan a neck pouch with the Seed artifact inside. "Keep this under your shirt," he whispered.

Alan wondered why Mup wanted him to bring it rather than keeping it at the camp, but he could read Mup's tone and decided against asking for now.

As Alan discreetly put on the neck pouch and tucked it into his shirt, he caught Mup doing the same. In Mup's neck pouch, Alan saw the outline of a pistol.

The trio said their goodbyes to Tier and Karjan and set out for the Heliop village. "If you catch a signal, don't leave this planet without me!" Zu called back to Tier.

The group arrived at the tree's boundary, where the jungle canopy below could be observed spreading far out across the crater floor. Still blanketed in the shadows of the crater walls, the jungle waited for sunlight. The pink sky had turned a light blue, and the sun was beginning its ascent—the birds of the forest had begun their ascents as well. Specks of movement darted above the canopy, and occasionally a larger creature, slow and lumbering, would begin a climb to air far above the jungle.

Walking along the trail, the group arrived at the garden of tall fruits. Only a few of the younger Heliops were at the garden, along with a pair of adults who were moving among the plants to inspect below their lower leaves. The children recognized Alan and ran over. They hesitated as they approached Mup and Zu.

The young Heliops signed a greeting timidly.

"Repeat the greeting," Alan instructed Mup and Zu. The two repeated the hand gesture, and the children squeaked in delight.

Alan signed: Men. Walk. Heliop. Home.

The Heliop children skipped in front of the group and led the way to the village.

The trio was surprised to find the village just as busy as when they had first encountered it the day before. All the adults were scattered around the village, carrying tools, piling leather skins near work pits, finishing breakfast, feeding the Heliosteeds.

The children ran ahead to a green, adult Heliop who was helping cut fruit for the Heliosteeds. They spoke with the adult excitedly and pointed to the trio. The Heliop stopped his work and approached Alan and the others with the children leading. The groups met near the Heliosteed paddock.

One of the children chittered to the green Heliop. The adult spoke back in a single-toned cheep.

Hello. Man, a child signed.

Alan replied in sign, a similar greeting.

The child showed a new sign for the adult's name and signed: Green. Fly.

"I think he is telling us this is a Heliosteed rider," Alan said.

"Ask him to show us the Heliosteeds or how they ride them," Mup interjected excitedly.

Alan thought for a moment and realized there was no sign for *watch* yet but tried a sign anyway. The child read the sign, and its ears perked up fully. It turned to Green and spoke in squeaks. The translation also startled Green, Alan judged. The child excitedly signed back to Alan: Yes.

Green and the children began walking to the Heliosteeds and looked for the group to follow.

"I have a feeling something was lost in translation," Mup chided as the group followed.

As they entered the paddock area, Green spoke to the other adult Heliosteed tenders. The group became visibly excited and looked over the men; then a few ran off to the leatherwork area and picked up a pile of completed leather straps and belts.

Green approached Zu, grabbed his wrist, and led him to a spotted Heliop throwing chopped fruit into a Heliosteed's enclosure. Green came back for Mup and similarly brought him to a Heliop in front of an enclosure. Last, Alan was led to the front of a caged Heliosteed. Only the child remained as a companion with Alan.

"Are we Heliosteed breakfast?" Mup asked with a nervous laugh.

The child signed: Man. Fly.

"Worse," Alan replied.

The group of Heliops returned with leather equipment and walked to Zu's paddock. Mup and Alan watched a nervous Zu. The spotted Heliop grabbed two sets of straps and belts, dropped one on the ground, and began sizing the other around Zu's waist.

Mup's head spun toward Alan, and a wide smiled erupted on his face. "No way!"

Zu, stunned with his arms raised to his shoulders, looked up from Spotted's sizing work and, in an alarmed tone, asked Alan, "We're not actually going flying, right?"

"I think we're committed," Alan said.

Zu's face went pale. "I'm not getting on that thing!"

"Where is your sense of adventure?" Alan swallowed as he watched Green sizing a belt around his waist. "This is field anthropology at its finest, right?"

"Tell them we just want to watch!" Zu exclaimed.

"Live a little!" Mup called to Zu. "Tomorrow we're space dust, remember?"

Green tightened the belt around Alan's hips. Alan grabbed Green's hand and let Green feel where his bony hips gave way to his fleshy side. Green loosened the belt and pulled it up over Alan's hips, then tightened it again. Green looked at the child and made a burst of chitters.

The child smiled at Alan.

"Hey, Mup, make sure the belt goes above your hips and is tightened. Check Zu too," Alan said.

"Why?"

"So if you go upside down, you don't slide out."

Mup smiled and wondered what important safety step the Heliops didn't yet understand for flying with men. He checked his belt and adjusted it. He helped Zu get similarly set up.

Green turned to the enclosure, unlatched it, and walked in. He motioned for Alan to follow.

The bird's shoulder was a foot above Alan's height, and the bird's head was six feet taller than that. The bird shuffled anxiously as the duo entered; it swiveled its head back and forth to alternate the eye it used to watch Alan.

The musky smell of the creature filled Alan's nose; its stuttered breathing barely audible over the pounding of Alan's heart in his ears. His focus narrowed, and he lost track of everything but the Heliosteed and Green.

Green expressed complete confidence with the creature as he approached it and ran his clawed paws through its feathers and along its body. The Heliosteed mirrored Alan's anxiety.

A fourth creature entered the paddock. The translation child entered wearing a belt and carrying a heavy load of tangled leather. He dropped the load on the ground and began working with Green to unravel the mess.

Alan watched closely and realized that the enormous pile of leather was two items: the bridle for the bird's head and a harness for the bird's body.

Green and the child quickly got the harness securely around the body of the Heliosteed. With the harness in place,

Green threw a strap over the bird's shoulder and used it to pull the nervous creature's head toward the ground. The two Heliops worked quickly to fasten the bridle on the animal's head. The work done, Green walked to the bird's prone shoulders and climbed on its back. He looked at Alan and motioned for him to mount the creature and sit behind him.

Alan hesitated, then moved toward the bird. Projecting false confidence, he climbed onto the bird. At first awkward, but ultimately successful, he sat on the creature's back with Green's head at his chest.

He felt a chunk of leather at his foot and realized the bird's harness had loops running alongside for stirrups. The stirrups were far too high, but he worked his feet into them nonetheless.

The child released the bird's head, and the Heliosteed rose to its feet. Alan began falling back but, gripping with his knees and leaning into Green, arrested the fall. Green chirped and fluttered his ears. He quickly found another set of stirrups that gave him leverage in the bird's standing position.

Green held two reins in his hands; they had been tied quickly to Green's belt while Alan had been attaching his own straps. The child Heliop suddenly appeared at Alan's side, grabbing at his clothes and climbing past him to take position between the reins in front of Green.

Alan leaned over and checked the group. Everyone was strapped in, Green holding the reins. How would the enclosure open?

Green whistled a loud, rising tone, and a Heliop outside the enclosure yanked a vine that pulled back the top of the enclosure. Alan looked up to see a clear blue sky above them.

In a burst of strength and with a dramatic thrust of giant wings, the Heliosteed leapt straight into the air and launched itself up through the opening in the enclosure.

As the Heliosteed worked into a vertical climb, Alan squeezed his legs tightly and leaned forward into Green, who himself was leaning into the child. Over his shoulder, he saw the plateau of the tree trunk fall away, the village at the edge getting smaller. The bird extended its wings fully and made another enormous thrust, pushing them even higher. Then, its wings folded in and its momentum upward stalled. The beast let its body fall over into a loop, and then the floating stall transitioned into a dive. Alan felt himself lift against the belt as a rising rush of wind swept over the bird and across his own body.

Looking ahead, straight down, he saw the tree trunk rising again and, beyond it, the jungle canopy. They rocketed past the village and plummeted at the canopy. Just as he became convinced a crash was imminent, the bird opened its wings and pulled out of the dive in a maneuver that made his eyes feel as heavy as rocks.

The bird was now level, skimming over the jungle canopy at high speed. The trio of riders sat up, the wind rippling through their hair. Alan looked around cautiously and realized they were stable... flying. A surge of excitement pulsed through his veins, and he raised his head to let out a whoop.

Green looked over his shoulder, his ears flattened in the wind, then turned back to focus ahead. Alan believed as if he had cheated death, and a feeling of relief chased away his anxieties. The maneuvering of takeoff shook out any fears.

He had not realized how tightly Green had kept the reins as he actively guided the Heliop on its journey over the jungle. Had Green guided the Heliop through their climb-and-dive maneuver, or did he simply control the timing? *Where did Green's guidance end and the Heliosteed's intuition begin?*

Green led the Heliosteed toward a large break in the jungle canopy ahead — the pit where the ships had been lost to the jungle monster.

The Heliosteed's glide was losing altitude. It was clear that Green was aiming for the pit, but it was not certain the bird would make it by gliding alone.

As if to signal to Alan their complete mastery of riding Heliosteeds, Green allowed the bird to sink closer to the canopy until the sound of leaves and branches whipping in the bird's downdraft became evident — and then the canopy disappeared to reveal the jungle pit.

Immediately, Alan could feel and smell a column of warm, putrid air rising from the pit. The bird gained altitude, despite remaining in a glide. Green, or the bird — it was not clear — began a graceful bank to remain in the column of air. As the beast's wings dipped, Alan got a glimpse of the massive decaying mess of the jungle squid rotting far below. Its skin had been totally removed, and now it was a nearly unrecognizable slop of gray-and-yellow meat.

He realized many other birds were also loitering in the rising air of the thermal. Some birds glided along nervously until Green's Heliosteed approached; then they would flap away to make space.

As the Heliosteed continued its rising arc, he found they had already soared a hundred feet above the jungle canopy in one-half lap around the edge of the pit. They were facing back toward where they had originated.

A line of six Heliosteeds, single-file, were skimming over the canopy toward the pit thermal. Alan watched carefully to see if he could see Zu or Mup. He found them, in the third and fourth spots. The other Heliosteeds were mounted by solo riders, two of which were carrying long, straight lances pointed upward.

Soon, the whole chain of Heliosteeds was within the thermal, all circling lazily on the rising elevator of warm air.

The spiral continued, the birds rising higher and higher — far higher than Alan thought was possible. They had risen above the surrounding crater walls and were reaching the base of small, thick clouds that were forming thousands of feet above the jungle as the morning air warmed up.

From their towering height, Alan could see the jungle extending in all directions past the crater walls — a plain of green dotted with shadows of clouds. It all resembled a peaceful sea of grass rather than the truth of the greedy, dangerous jungle.

As they approached the base of a cloud, Green pulled the Heliosteed out of its spiral and aimed him straight toward the east.

It occurred to Alan the beast had only flapped its wings three times in the entire flight.

The other Heliosteeds turned to follow Green as they reached the cloud base. Quietly, the train of creatures glided high over the crater valley.

For twenty minutes, the creatures continued on until they passed high over the mountain walls of the crater boundary. Trees covered the peaks, but in rare areas, raw, yellow rock cut through, jagged like a serrated knife, while in other areas softly smoothed.

Once past the peaks, Green had the beast enter a steep dive parallel to the outside crater wall. They quickly passed below the crest of the wall, and at mid-height, Green steered them back toward the mountains. As they approached the rising terrain, Alan could feel an updraft of air lifting the group. They rode the updraft along the face of the mountain until they approached a few hundred feet from a yellow stone outcropping at the peak. Green pulled the beast's reins, and for the first time since leaving the paddock, the Heliosteed began flapping its wings. The bird slowed down and landed gracefully on a flat slab of rock centered at the top of the crater wall.

The Heliosteed dropped to its belly, and the Heliop riders untied their belts and slid off the bird. Alan followed, his legs aching.

His feet touched solid rock for the first time in many days. A strong, persistent breeze curled over the ridge, and he considered that the bird may have lain down to find relief from the buffeting wind.

Green and the child stretched their legs and walked the perimeter of the rock. Of the nearby pitches, only the stone they stood on was flat. It was long and wide enough to accommodate dozens of Heliosteeds. The others were vertical knives of granite piercing out of a jungle.

Just as he realized they were alone, the next Heliosteed arrived. Its sole rider unstrapped itself and leapt to the rock. Green welcomed the new rider, and the two begun chittering between themselves.

The child looked toward Alan. Its ears were half-open, perhaps tired and sore from being folded down for the length of the ride.

Man. Fly.

Alan replied: Yes. Man. Fly.

Alan smiled as he took in his surroundings. The view from the vista was overwhelming. Jungle valley in one direction, a plain of endless rainforest in the other, and jagged rock monoliths to either side along the crest of the mountain ridge. The prone Heliosteeds, monstrous creatures, were hiding from a mountain wind while their riders socialized.

The next Heliosteed brought two riders, Mup and a yellow Heliop. Mup confidently untied himself and dismounted the bird.

Walking toward Alan, Mup exclaimed, "I don't think I'll ever see flying the same way!" Mup gave him a slap on the back. "You looked great up there!"

"After that first dive, I realized it couldn't get any scarier," Alan replied with a smile.

Another Heliosteed carrying Zu and his spotted pilot appeared from below the wall edge and landed. Zu clumsily untangled himself from the leather reins and dismounted.

"If I ever got to tell anyone that I rode a huge bird with a giant rat, I don't think they would believe me," Zu said. He paused for a moment. "I think I need to sit down."

* * *

The group of men and Heliops sat together in a mixed line along the leeward side of the rock overlooking the crater. A solo Heliop rider had brought a satchel of food for the group, and he pulled out each item and passed it down the line. Mup, at the other end of the group, prepared the dehydrated lunch he had brought in the backpack. When completed, the entire line of riders and men exchanged food up and down the row.

"Is it safe to eat?" Mup asked as an open fruit arrived in his hands. Zu and Alan were already chewing their share.

"Sure, I guess. What does it matter, really?" Alan offered out of the side of his mouth before swallowing.

Last meal, Alan thought.

The Heliops expressed no similar hesitation in drinking the salty meat soup the men offered.

Alan accepted nearly all the food the Heliops brought: fruit of all colors and textures, meat from animals large and small, live insects wrapped in leaves, and more. But he passed on what looked like a sack of sentient eyeballs that turned and blinked.

As the group finished the last of the food, he realized that the independent conversations from the Heliops and the men had stopped, and silence had fallen over the band of travelers.

For a long while, the silence was unbroken, until finally, the Heliop at the end of the line retrieved a cone of bark from his satchel and stood.

The child leaned forward and waved at Alan, then signed: Ceto. Man. See.

The standing Heliop breathed deeply and blew into the cone; a whistle with a sibling tone of bass filled the air. The tone blew steadily, then rose sharply and silenced.

The group of Heliops all stood. Sensing ceremony, the men looked at each other and stood as well.

The end Heliop blew the horn, this time in a steady, slow rhythm. High chitters and foreign keys joined the horn as the other Heliops began singing.

From behind the opposite wall of the crater, dozens of miles in the distance, a sliver of light rose like a second sun.

Ceto, the sibling planet, was rising.

As the Heliops saw it, they sang louder until the whole chorus turned into frenzied dancing and slapping of their hands. At the crescendo, the song ended, and the group began running to their Heliosteeds. Green and the child motioned for the men to follow.

As Alan turned to run back to the Heliosteeds, he was stunned to see, on the opposite horizon, out over the endless plain of the jungle, there was now a tremendous line of dark, boiling clouds a hundred miles away. The base of the clouds was beneath the horizon, but Alan could tell that light would not reach the jungle below them. The peaks of the clouds stretched high into the atmosphere and were enormous, erupting mountains of rising moisture. An incredible storm had moved in silently and was approaching.

The groups swiftly mounted their birds and tied themselves in. Alan, startled with the sudden change of mood, quickly yanked at his belt once it was fixed to make sure it was truly on tight. He squeezed the bird hard with his legs and awaited Green's piloting. Green pulled the prone Heliosteed to a stand. The mountain wind pushed into their backs. Green looked over his shoulder, cheeped, and pulled at the reins of the bird, causing it to launch itself into flight.

This time, the bird immediately dove over the edge of the rock and began flapping furiously. Alan immediately sensed the air was turbulent and tumbling wildly. Despite the bird's frantic flapping, the group was losing altitude quickly. Green was having the bird go for distance, not altitude, Alan realized.

The bird sprinted forward with increasing speed and, as the turbulence subsided, began gaining altitude.

Alan looked over his shoulder and saw that the Heliosteeds behind were following the same chaotic flight path. However, soon the group was flying a thousand feet above the canopy in a gentle journey back to the center of the crater valley. A set of thrusts with flapping wings and a long glide. Another set of thrusts and another long glide.

Green looked over his shoulder and reached behind his back to grab Alan's hands. Pulling them past his sides, Green placed Alan's hands on the reins. Alan could feel the tension on the straps lessen as Green let Alan take over. The fluttering of the leather in the wind jostled his hands, but Alan tightened his grip and pulled back slightly. The bird bumped up momentarily but did not climb. Green pulled the reins and leaned back — the bird rose.

So, there are two inputs — the reins and the weight of the rider.

Green guided Alan through gentle maneuvers to both sides and through gentle changes of angle. Alan was surprised that the bird was difficult to fly only in that it tended to resist changes and ignored subtle commands. The bird read its rider's intentions and responded only to clearly intentioned commands — it ignored Alan's occasional mistake of using the rein as a support for adjusting his seating.

Green pointed to his feet and showed Alan how he used them to command the bird to perform more extreme maneuvers — the feet acting as an emphasis on the command. Green dug a foot in on one side and leaned while pulling the rein, and the bird turned in a deep bank. The turn complete, Green signaled to Alan with a sideways glance to repeat the maneuver.

Continuing the turn, the bird banked until it reached their original heading.

Bird and rider are a team, Alan thought. *It won't let me do something stupid.*

From their left, a Heliosteed appeared, flapping its wings to gain altitude. The bird pitched into a graceful, diving arc that passed in front of and below Alan's Heliosteed. Mup was piloting.

Green pointed to Mup, looked over his shoulder at Alan, and squeaked.

Here goes nothing.

Alan commanded the Heliosteed into a diving bank, and intuitively the creature knew to chase after Mup. Air rushed across Alan's face as he suddenly found the tops of the jungle trees filling his vision before him — Mup's Heliosteed a few hundred feet in advance.

Alan's Heliosteed had a competitive spirit and aggressively increased its speed with strong thrusts of its wings. As they caught up, Alan leaned back and gently pulled on the reins.

It's not a race.

The Heliosteed put itself behind and to the side of Mup and copied every maneuver Mup commanded. The two creatures flew as a duet in an elegant aerial dance.

A third Heliosteed arrived in the formation, Zu holding the reins. Alan waved, and Zu returned.

"Mup!" Alan shouted. "Race you to that cloud!"

Before Mup could reply, Zu's Heliosteed lurched forward to take the lead. Alan urged his ride to pick up speed, and the creature released itself from trailing Mup and sprinted forward.

The pilots were no longer in control; the Heliosteeds were all racing each other. Green and the other Heliops did their part to speed up by reducing their profile. Alan used the straps to give guidance to the Heliosteed, showing the cloud as the goal of the race.

A thousand feet left, Mup and Zu had pulled out ahead. Mup's Heliosteed vanished first into the cloud, followed quickly by Zu.

Alan's Heliosteed entered the cloud, and the temperature quickly changed to a cool breeze. He felt mist accumulate on his skin.

As suddenly as they had entered the cloud, they emerged from it, and the jungle spread out far below. The race over, the Heliosteeds slowly turned to reverse course and rejoin the main group.

When they had all linked up again, Mup and Alan flew side-by-side.

"I'm already a better pilot!" Mup shouted.

"I'm not sure the bird agrees!" Alan shouted back. "It's the one doing all the hard work!"

Suddenly, through the gentle sound of air flowing past, came a shrill shriek, unmistakably from the mouth of a Heliop. Without a moment's hesitation, Green grabbed the reins and yanked to the left, commanding the bird into a violent dive. Reflexively, Alan grabbed at Green for stability, and as he did, from the periphery of his vision, he saw a tremendous dark shape dive through the air they had just been in.

Green yanked again, and the Heliosteed rolled into a corkscrew flight that left Alan entirely disoriented as sky and jungle traded places in a rapid series of rolls.

When the maneuver ended, in front of them, a dark bird three times the size of any Heliosteed was in a dramatic, deep bank, turning to fly toward Alan's Heliosteed head-on.

Green glanced quickly over his shoulder, then had the Heliosteed pull into a shallow climb and bank aggressively to reverse course. In the center of their turn, two Heliosteeds passed a few feet over Alan's head in a straight line toward the attacking monster, each rider carrying a long lance.

The two Heliosteeds flapped furiously on a direct course for the flying monster as their riders lowered their lances into attack position. The creatures all closed in at a tremendous speed, and in a sudden flurry of wings and shapes, the three converged. Both Heliosteeds shot out of the entanglement, one going up, the other going down. A lance tumbled on a freefall toward the jungle, the other lance lodged loosely in the monster's body.

Still, the dark creature headed for Alan.

Green glanced over his shoulder and saw that the beast was tailing him, then snapped his Heliosteed into a sharp, banking turn to reverse course toward the creature. *Toward him!* Alan thought.

The tight turn made Alan feel heavy and as if he would lose his grip on the back of the bird. When they emerged from the turn, the attacking creature was dropping a set of six legs to pluck Green's Heliosteed out of the air. Just as the two were about to crash, the Heliosteed descended abruptly in a sharp dive, then pulled back up on the other side of the monster. Closing the distance had sharply increased the relative speed of Alan's Heliosteed, and the monster hadn't been able to catch the darting prey.

Now the creature was banking around to continue chase. Behind it, Alan could see the other Heliosteeds spread out and flying above the fray. The two defending Heliosteeds had joined the group and were furiously getting into a position directly above the monster but out of reach if it changed the object of its attention.

The monster was catching up with Alan's Heliosteed. No matter how hard it pushed to open up distance the Heliosteed was simply overloaded with riders.

The group of high-flying Heliosteeds flew in a shallow dive to get ahead of the monster. When in position, they rolled into a dive and swooped across the monster's path, the Heliosteed swiping at the dark creature's head.

Green put the Heliosteed into another dive, and the monster matched. The jungle canopy drew closer, and soon there would be no more room to drop or maneuver.

A terrible howl shot through the air and rumbled Alan's body — the beast was just a moment away from reaching out with its jaws and capturing the fleeing Heliosteed.

The defending Heliosteeds dived, futilely harassing the creature.

A third Heliosteed dropped out of the sky, two riders on its back. Needles of plasma shot out from a pistol wielded by the passenger, missing wildly, but quickly correcting and finding their mark across the monster's body.

The creature jolted, drew its wings in, and rolled, snapping its jaws at the plasma shots as if they were an attacking creature. Mup continued the barrage of shots until his pilot was forced to pull out of the dive and climb past the beast.

The monster dropped and collided with the canopy in an explosive cloud of leaves and branches, its body tumbling wildly and disappearing. Alan watched as the crash site got farther and farther behind. The monster appeared once more from the jungle, awkwardly struggling to rise above the canopy. It opened its wings, rising partially out of the trees until a swarm of creatures leapt from all directions onto the beast and it disappeared back into the jungle.

A Heliosteed dropped in from above and kept position off Alan's right side—Mup and the yellow Heliop. Mup waved his pistol.

The rest of the flight home, the group flew in a dispersed arrangement low over the treetops as Ceto rose over the mountains. This was the sibling planet's final approach, and as it rose, it felt to Alan as if it would fill the entire sky.

Chapter 11
Tier

In the morning light, Tier and Karjan watched Zu, Alan, and Mup walk to the Heliop village for the day. "If you catch a signal, don't leave this planet without me!" Zu called back to Tier.

When the group had rounded behind a monolith of wood, out of sight, Tier and Karjan walked back to where the beacon and drones were kept.

Karjan took the beacon off its high ledge and turned it over, checking its diagnostic panel and placing it back into position. He connected to the device with his computer and scrolled through its status.

"There is nothing out there that the beacon's heard. It's not picking up any communications other than noise from the two ships in the pit that still have some functioning computers," Karjan said.

"Stay here with the beacon then," Tier replied. "It's important that if anything passes through the system, you're here to let them know it's not a fluke."

"You'll work the drones?" Karjan asked.

"No, I need you to do that too," Tier said. "I'm heading back down into the jungle to see about Rell and Sybus. Let them know we made camp and are running the beacon under clear sky."

"Are you going to bring them back up?"

"If Rell can walk some—maybe."

"I hope he can. I wouldn't want them to stay in that jungle another night."

"They are just as sharp as you. I'm sure they will be fine," Tier said.

Tier grabbed a pistol and holstered it on his hip as he snatched a small pack he had put medicine into.

"If I'm not back by sunset, I've decided to stay with them, and I'll come back in the morning."

* * *

Tier found that downclimbing the tree was more difficult than he had expected. Even with the abundance of crevices to rest in, the routine of blindly searching for footholds wore on his physical and mental energy. He continued his descent and entered the jungle canopy, surrounded by the noise of bugs and birds, audible but invisible. Reaching lower and lower into the green mess, a tangled pathway of branches and limbs that could serve as a guide appeared.

Once on the network of limbs, he looked down and saw an incredible lattice of jungle vegetation. If he slipped and could not catch himself on the first branch, he would certainly die tumbling down between the limbs before ever coming to a rest on whatever surface was far below.

The impressions the group's feet had left on the moss were gone, but other clues of the group's passing remained: stripped bark, a vine in an unnatural position, branches bent awkwardly. As he followed the clues, he felt a sense of satisfaction as Mup's navigation markers appeared, confirming Tier's tracking skills.

As he passed through leaves that hung over the path, bugs clung to his clothes and found their way to his skin, biting him. When he slapped them, his hand came back with a bit of bug and a bit of sweat.

Every creature can smell me, and anything that is hungry is following me. I hate these forests, this heat, these creatures. There is no sense of rhythm and equilibrium in the wild here — just kill or be killed. Everything out for itself. Everything fighting. No sense, just action and reaction in one mess.

His mind wandered to his home, the long stretches of dry grasslands that extended for a thousand miles without water. Gold seas of grass in a flat plain the size of oceans. Within the grass oceans, few animals survived, and no person settled. To cross required patience, wisdom, and teamwork—it was a battle of person and environment.

The land, the grasslands, was the most patient and cruel opponent. Yet, the land was predictable and governed by rules that could be learned and passed on between generations. At home, everything followed a rhythm and order. Everything had its place and role.

Deeper into the jungle Tier descended. Going down was always more difficult than climbing—more ways to slip and less to hold on to.

A false vine jerked to grab ahold of him, but he was quicker than the plant and jumped free before it could ensnare him. The vine coiled unevenly, jumping, writhing, and slithering upward like a snake without a head.

Tier continued down, moving from limb to limb. He stopped frequently to listen for changes in the jungle, to listen for telltale signs of stalkers in the shade.

The sunlight that was obscured by hundreds of feet of foliage above was shining in from the side—a sign that he was getting closer to the walls of the jungle pit.

A glint of metal caught his attention a hundred feet below and ahead. *Certainly some of the crates the crew had unloaded from the ship before it fell into the pit.* The two crewmates would be nearby.

Swinging down from a vine, he landed on the flat, solid surface of a mega tree limb, the same limb that the ships had landed on and that had been snapped by the pit monster.

The small camp, a cluster of metal crates, had been pillaged. The crates were split open and tossed about, their contents spilling out across the camp. His gaze followed the debris and moved to the branches and limbs surrounding it. Black scorch marks pocked a vertical limb and some of its neighbors. He saw evidence of a struggle in the foliage—

something large had been here. Unmoving, he scanned the jungle slowly for signs of the crewmen.

A man's foot hung over the crotch in a limb above the campsite. Tier ran to the limb and climbed it with the help of a nearby vine. Ten feet up, he found Rell lying awkwardly on the limb, his legs cast and haphazardly splinted with shafts from the crates and his shirt soaked through with sweat.

"Tier," Rell said softly, "I heard something climbing the vine, and I thought my death was here. I'm glad it's you. I am so cold."

"What happened? Where is Sybus?"

Rell glanced in the direction of the camp beyond his feet and swallowed. "A brood of... things... came in the night, and Sybus fought them while I climbed this tree. I didn't see him after, but I heard the creatures down there go back into the jungle."

Tier stared at Rell. His pain, physical and emotional, was clear. He had been alone all night, scared. Tier grabbed his water from his belt and put it in Rell's hands.

It was a stupid idea to leave Rell and Sybus. We should have taken them or stayed here with them.

"I'm sorry," Tier said. "I shouldn't have left."

"We needed the beacon up there. And you came back." Rell winced and grabbed at his leg.

"Your legs, worse?"

"Yes — and a bite. One of those things must have gotten at me. I get shakes in waves. It started when I felt a burning on the back of my leg, and now I feel tingling everywhere. I am so cold, Tier."

Tier put a hand on Rell's forehead. He was hot to the touch.

"I'll get you something to cover up with. Do you need food?"

"Yes. Thank you."

Tier slid down the vine and began working through the mess surrounding the crates. The spread debris was mostly excavation gear and electronics, but a camping crate had been in the mix. He kicked through its contents and found a blanket. Most of the food was gone, but an energy bar was left undiscovered.

Climbing the vine, he wondered how Rell had also managed to do so with broken legs.

"Here, I found a blanket and some food," Tier said as he climbed into the tree. He shook the blanket and threw it over Rell, who grasped at it and held it close to his body, hiding under it. Rell closed his eyes and lay quietly, his teeth chattering.

Rell is poisoned, severely. There is no way he is going to survive — I don't even know what kind of animal bit him. The medkit — perhaps I could use a sedation and fever reducer?

He removed his backpack and produced the medical kit. It was sparse and contained only the blunt instruments of medicine — the basics for cuts, infections, stomach sickness, insect bites, fevers. But it did contain a set of powerful painkillers and sedatives.

"Here, swallow this. And I'm going to give you something to numb the pain." Tier handed Rell a pill, and as Rell lifted his head to swallow it, Tier pushed a microsyringe against Rell's arm and injected sedative.

Rell's eyes opened wide, and then they slowly returned to a sleepy gaze.

"I can... really feel... that," Rell stammered.

"Yeah, it's a painkiller and sedative. It's strong stuff," Tier said as he packed the medical kit.

"Pellia?"

"Yeah."

"Thank the Maker for Pellia."

Tier watched as Rell lay still. His teeth ceased chattering, and Rell finally looked at peace.

"I wish I was home," Rell said.

"Yes, so do I," Tier replied softly.

Rell turned his head to face Tier but did not open his eyes. "When I was young, really young, they had us read Marshata. Did you read Marshata?"

"I think we all did."

"Well, it was my favorite. It was everything about our home, our people, our culture... in one text."

"This is why we all read it."

Rell continued, "What I liked about Marshata was she knew so early in her life what her purpose was — like a star that she followed every night, unwaveringly. She understood how important it was to preserve our ways and that it took effort — effort to keep it from unraveling into chaos. It was like tending a garden, a daily ritual, a chore and so often a joy. She understood the whole of it and dedicated her life to it. The fight against the Grii and the High to protect the grass oceans. Building the elder homes. The founding of the Mission."

Tier interrupted, "And because she did all that, we still have something to preserve today."

Rell smiled, eyes closed. "As the Maker taught."

"As the Maker taught," Tier replied.

"I knew," Rell continued slowly, "that I wanted to be in the Mission. To be like Marshata, and to protect and preserve, even as the galaxy got smaller. I joined the Mission out of primary —"

"Young," Tier said.

"Just the right age — all energy. My first assignment was to be an ambassador's detail on trips to the Core. It was... Ambassador Forn. She was very experienced and well regarded by the Mission. She often went to the Core and did well to keep our home prosperous but safe. She prayed every day on schedule—never skipped. Very devout. She had a husband, and he kept the three kids.

"When we traveled, she kept a copy of Marshata with her. I think she was inspired by Marshata the way I was. She was good to me. She gave me her time and advice.

"Once, when returning from the Core, we were at a way station transferring to the last jump. The station was like all other way stations, crowded—unsafe. Someone came at her with a knife, and I stopped him before he could strike her. He got close enough to cut her jacket."

Rell paused, tired. He pulled the blanket up under his neck.

"After that, she requested I be her main detail. A high honor for a kid like me. I felt like I had achieved the peak of my career in my first assignment.

"We went to the Core very frequently for trade work. She was always attending to trade to make sure we had access to the markets.

"We stayed at the same building on Devro—an enormous white pillar near the Diplomatic Square. I had the room across from hers.

"One night, very late, I heard her door close, and I checked. She always had everyone come to my room first, and then I would escort them to her room. Maybe the door closing was her leaving? But she always stayed inside. I messaged her, and she said she was fine.

"A while later I heard laughing: her and a man from her room." Rell paused. "I don't think I would ever be alone at night with another woman if I were married.

"Soon, I heard a crash, and she did not respond, so I went into her room. She was with the man; I did not recognize him, and the two were naked and unconscious. They were both in comas from a local drug."

Tier watched as Rell thought. His voice was slowing.

"The doctor said she had become addicted over many months and finally had too much. I was shocked. Horrified. I was ashamed. I had spent five years protecting someone so…"

"Weak," Tier answered.

Rell nodded and swallowed. "Weak. She was no Marshata. She betrayed her husband, her children… our people. In the end, she brought shame to everyone around her.

"The Mission reassigned me to work with you. The work is important—but I don't think I will see my contribution. I won't…" Rell's voice trailed off. "Know if my contribution mattered."

Tier touched Rell's hair and pulled it out of his face. "Do you remember the proverb of the Torches?"

"No," Rell said quietly, his eyes still closed.

"The proverb says that generations of men and women will each carry a torch forward. They will give the flame from their torch to their children, and they to theirs. Along the way, the weak and unfocused will lose their flame. Those without flame will become greater in number, and many will question the very importance of the flame. But in many generations, a time of great need will arise, and one child whose family has kept their flame alive will save the people. One unbroken chain of dedication."

Rell lay quietly as he took in Tier's story. "The chain of torches. I always wondered where that saying came from."

"Your torch is alight, Rell," Tier said softly. "I've seen that in you since we met. Your work has never been in vain; you have inspired us with your flame and passed it on."

"Thank you," Rell breathed.

Tier opened the medkit and reloaded the syringe with Pellia. He uncovered Rell's arm and injected it.

Rell did not react. His eyes stayed closed as his muscles released, his head tilted back, and his breathing slowly faded and stopped.

Chapter 12
Understanding

A lan helped pull the top of the Heliosteed enclosure shut and walked out, Green following. A crowd of Heliops had surrounded, watching, and as they emerged, they chittered, danced, and reached out to lay hands on Green.

The other Heliops from the flight received similar treatments — adulations and song — from the crowd of excited Heliops. The trio of human riders waded through the crowd.

"Thank you!" Alan shouted as he threw his arms over Mup. "I'm never going anywhere without you ever again!" he continued with a smile.

"I'm glad my pilot got an angle for a shot. We came in on that steep dive, I was worried I was going to blast my Heliop's big head!"

Zu smiled. "You almost had a chance to meet that beast's children for dinner."

The crowds of Heliops had decorated the pilots with necklaces of nuts, flowers, and shards of reddish metal.

"What do you suppose that's all about?" Mup asked. "It certainly wasn't their first flight. They really know how to work with those birds."

The group watched the raucous crowd.

"It must have something to do with the ceremony on the rock, when Ceto rose," Alan said.

"Indeed," Zu replied.

The child Heliop broke out from the crowd and walked up to Alan. The child signed: Man. Food. Village.

"I think they want us to join them for dinner," Alan said.

Mup hesitated. "I'm sorry, Alan. I've got plans tonight," he said.

Zu and Alan stared blankly at Mup.

"I'm kidding. Of course. Maybe they have drinks here." Mup slapped Alan's shoulder.

* * *

Alan and Mup walked along the edge of the tree, behind the village. The sky had turned bright pink from the setting sun, but the looming planet of Ceto was brightly lit — light reflecting off its oceans and landing like a noon sun. The pair observed the surface of the planet, close enough to see details normally only visible in a descent from orbit.

On the horizon before them, behind the border mountains of the crater, enormous clouds approached. The tops were high enough to be bathed in brilliant white light, the middle layers a dark pink, and the lowest portion of the approaching line an ominous gray — occasionally sparkling blue and white with lightning.

Alan and Mup felt a hint of dizziness, as if the tree were swaying slowly and deeply beneath their feet. Across the jungle in front of them, the trees lightly rippled and swayed as well. The animals of the jungle, normally settling for the night, were not quieting — they were screeching and calling loudly from below the treetops.

"Something is happening," Mup said quietly among the sea of jungle noises.

"Nothing feels right," Alan agreed. "The tree is — *swaying*. Everything is unsettled."

"Listen," Mup said.

The two strained to hear a sound beneath all the other noise — a constant low-pitched rumble. Mup approached the edge of the tree and looked down. "It's coming from the jungle," he said.

Alan moved closer to the edge cautiously. The sound of rushing water rumbled far below.

"Water," Alan said. "But no rain. Where could it…" He trailed off. "It's a tide. Ceto is pulling water in a tide."

"We get to see firsthand something no one ever gets to see," Mup said, looking at Alan.

From the village a sharp drum began beating rhythmically; more followed, and a complex pattern emerged. Singing and whistling joined in.

"Do you think they know this is the end?" Mup asked as they turned to watch the crowd of Heliops on the opposite side of the village.

"If they know, they're taking it well. If they don't know, I wouldn't tell them. I'd rather be them right now—not knowing," Alan said.

The Heliops broke into a communal dance, swaying and jumping together. From behind the crowd, Alan could make out the silhouette of three human figures.

"Zu, Tier, and Karjan are back," Alan said as he walked toward the crowd. "And by the looks of them, the beacon didn't bring us anyone."

Mup stopped Alan, a hand on this shoulder.

"Alan." Mup swallowed. "Tier and Karjan are hiding something."

Alan furrowed his brows and tilted his head. "What could they be hiding—here, now?"

"I don't know, but last night when we were talking—there is more to them than what they let us see."

"Do you think Zu knows?"

"I am sure they are hiding it from Zu too, whatever it is."

"Wow," Alan said, his skepticism wearing off. "I didn't see that."

"Just be careful. Be careful around them."

Alan read Mup, saw his seriousness, and nodded. "Yeah, of course, thanks."

* * *

As the pink sky gave way to a clear view of Ceto, the Heliops continued to dance and celebrate. Occasionally, a Heliop would be selected and thrown into the air by the other Heliops over and over. At the end of the ritual, an older pair of Heliops would approach the celebrated Heliop and offer two large leather satchels, joined by a set of leather straps. The three would embrace while the crowd whistled and sang.

Alan watched the performance repeated; every Heliop who had piloted a Heliosteed to the rock was included, and a handful of others as well. *This must be a rite of passage*, he thought.

In the sky above, faintly at first, curtains of green and purple light appeared, moving quickly in streaks away from Ceto. Like bolts of lightning, a charge of green would flash on the horizon and spread in all directions, zipping across the sky. The show became increasingly intense until the auroras colored the village and all the Heliops in a pastel glow.

As he watched the lights, a group of children found him and pulled at his shirt. They urged him to follow, and he let himself be guided. They led him to a work pit for leather that now had fruit lining its edges.

The children signed: Alan. Heliop. Food. Village.

Alan, unsure, signed: Yes.

The children, amused, patted the ground as they all settled into squats. *A dinner with children*, he realized.

The children had formed a bond with him. The signs were known only by the children and Alan, and it made it feel like a secret club—at least to him.

He sat on the edge of the work pit ledge and took a bite of a fruit that had been cubed.

Alan got the children's attention, mimed the dancing of the Heliops, and made a sign to show its meaning. The children chittered and waved their ears in what he appreciated as the equivalent of laughter and delight.

He continued in sign: Heliops. Dance. Question.

The children signed: Yes. Dance.

Another child continued the signs: Heliops. Fly. More. Villages. Night.

Flying and villages? They are flying away to other villages tonight. Migrating? Perhaps the younger generation is migrating to other villages – to find mates?

He breathed out with the realization. A ceremony to bid the youth farewell on their new lives.

They don't know what's coming, he realized.

A tightness grabbed his throat—a sadness, which moved him to stare blankly to the ground.

The creatures watched Alan silently, their glassy eyes unmoving. The man-creature was upset, not angry—in pain.

Alan felt the weight of a metal object he had been carrying under his shirt in the neck pouch. He raised his head and touched the pouch through his shirt.

Time to ask the real question.

He pulled the pouch awkwardly out through the neck of his shirt.

The Heliops cooed and shuffled closer, intrigued by the mystery of the object.

Alan removed from the pouch a flat, cloth-wrapped rectangle. He placed the object on the ground in front of his feet and unwrapped the cloth to reveal the gleaming blue-red metal of Mup's artifact.

The youths erupted in squeals and competed to invent a sign for the artifact. After a moment, the group settled on a flat hand-chopping perpendicularly into another hand to represent the artifact.

He signed to the youths: Artifact. More. Question.

The youths squeaked wildly, their ears quivering and the lot exchanging glances at each other. They pointed toward the village and signed: Yes. Artifact. More.

Alan again signed: Artifact. More. Question.

The youths stood and pointed in all different directions.

He repeated: Artifact. More. Question.

The repeat of the question confused the Heliops, and they made the same reply less enthusiastically.

He signed: Artifact. More. Question.

The youths stared at him. Cautiously, a Heliop child stood, looked at Alan, and answered: Artifact. More. Rain.

The other Heliops looked to the child, then looked at Alan. They repeated: Artifact. More. Rain.

Rain?

The standing child moved through the crowd, picked up the artifact, and dropped it again. He looked up to the sky and signed: Artifact. More. Rain.

Oh my God.

Alan stared at the child and signed: Artifact. Home. Question.

Silently, all the Heliop children looked toward the looming planet of Ceto and pointed.

The child signed: Artifact. Home. Ceto.

Chapter 13
Truth

The winds from the south had intensified and brought a sudden downpour of rain. The violent onslaught of water hadn't stopped the Heliops from celebrating. The warm air became even more humid, and Alan felt as if he were swimming as he ran through the village, weaving between groups of dancing Heliops. He found the group of men clustered under a sagging leather awning, streams of water pouring over the side.

"What a storm!" Zu said.

"The planets aren't colliding!" Alan shouted over the sound of splashing water, his clothes soaked and his hair matted to his head. "Helios and Ceto aren't ending tonight!"

"What?" Mup replied, shocked.

"The planets aren't crashing! Their atmospheres will link—the two planets will brush by—but they aren't crashing!"

The group looked at each other. "How... why?" Zu stuttered.

"The Heliops we flew with are *migrating* to Ceto— tonight! They are flying the Heliosteeds to the other planet! This is a farewell party—they've done this before! This is a *ritual* because it's happened before! The pieces fit!"

The group looked over the Heliop celebration in the rain. The Heliops knew what was going to happen—they knew the truth.

Zu smiled, and a wave of relief washed over his face.

"The artifacts," Alan continued, "what we came for. They are on Ceto. The artifacts come from Ceto. What we are looking for is on—"

"Ceto," Zu finished.

With a yelp of joy, Mup ran out into the crowd of Heliops and began dancing with the sopping-wet creatures.

Tier looked at Alan. "The artifacts are from Ceto?"

"They are all over the forest. They fall like rain when the two planets pass. The storm that is coming here... it's also up there!" Alan pointed to Ceto.

The group stepped out from underneath the awning and looked up. Half of the sky was still clear from the towering mass of clouds that was pouring rain—and in the open sky were the colorful shocks of auroras and the surface of Ceto high overhead.

A massive swirling storm system was visible on Ceto's surface, and it was rising—rising off Ceto and into space, the space that was meeting Helios. The two planets' storm systems were combining.

"The storms pull debris off the surfaces of the planets, and they rain on each other in a giant exchange," Alan continued.

Mup returned, out of breath. "I am going to dance with those little rats in the rain forever!"

"We leave tonight—with the Heliops who are flying across," Alan said.

The group was shocked. Mup's smile disappeared.

"What? For all's sake, why?" Karjan exclaimed.

"The Heliops are insistent that we have to leave tonight if we want to see the artifacts' origin." Alan paused and caught his breath. He swallowed and looked at the group.

"This morning, I woke up knowing that today was my last day," Alan said. "Now I know it's not. I am not going to waste another moment. I'm not going to sit anymore and wait for opportunities. This is it—this is the opportunity. We know where to go, and we know how to get there, and we know what we are looking for," —Alan pointed to Ceto—"is there. It happens tonight! I'm going to Ceto to finish what we came here to do!"

Tier spoke up. "Hold on, let's think about this for a second."

Zu interrupted. "Alan's right. We're here, and we've come this far. We cross over while we have this chance."

"I'm in," Mup said with little thought.

"So, we just hitch a ride? Then what?" Tier objected. "Marooned on Ceto forever? Search parties are going to look for us on Helios—not Ceto."

"We fly on our own Heliosteeds," Mup replied.

"And bring the beacon in case we get stuck on Ceto," Zu added.

"But we have to get going *now*," Alan said. "We have to collect our things and —"

Tier and Karjan were shocked. "*Fly our own Heliosteeds? How can we fly —*"

"We can fly," Zu replied.

"Some things happened today," Alan said.

Tier and Karjan looked at the group, finding themselves suddenly on the outside.

Alan continued, "We have to get back to camp, grab everything, and bring it here. We'll need to pack what we're taking and trade the rest for the rides."

"We got to get back before they leave!" Mup shouted and began running toward camp, the others turning to follow.

"Come help carry!" Zu shouted to Tier as he ran away down the path. "Or stay here and trade for food! I don't care!"

As the three ran for camp, Tier and Karjan stood in the rain. Tier watched as the men dashed away, set on their journey. There was no stopping them on this. He looked at Karjan. "We don't have a choice. We will go along as we are required."

* * *

Alan was retrieving his gear from a nook where he had hidden it away when Tier and Karjan came into camp.

The pack would be difficult to load on the Heliosteed; it could unbalance him unless he slung it in front of himself. He realized he knew little about packing a Heliosteed, and a moment of doubt fell over him.

This morning I thought I was dead.

The rifle Alan had brought caught his eye. They would be difficult to carry and dangerous to leave behind.

Mup saw Alan contemplating the weapon in the rain. "We'll take its battery with us."

Alan agreed and popped loose the energy cartridge, tucking it into the bag and hiding the rifle in a hole in the tree's surface.

"The beacon," Zu called to Tier as he arrived. "The most important thing is the beacon."

Tier and Karjan moved directly to the small case they had carefully hidden. Karjan pulled it out and set about unlocking it. Tier produced an empty backpack, sturdy and waterproof. The case clicked, and Karjan opened it carefully. Satisfied with the contents, he closed it again.

Tier looked around the camp and saw that all the men were occupied with collecting their belongings. He nodded to Karjan, and Karjan carefully stuffed the crate into the backpack. The two worked the seals of the pack until they closed fully. Tier hefted up the bag onto Karjan, who pulled the straps over his shoulders and pulled them to fit snugly.

Tier walked over to the beacon, sitting high on a natural shelf, and brought it down. The small, white device had still not registered any signals.

"The beacon," Tier called to Zu. "Got it." He placed the beacon in its case and put the closed case in his own backpack to bring along.

The group of men returned to the village. It had been difficult to find in the pouring rain, but even through the storm, they could hear the sound of drumming. Each carrying a pack, they entered the village and waded through the dancing crowds. They made their way to the awning and piled their bags.

"Now what?" Mup asked.

"The hard part," Alan said. "Figuring out how to get three Heliosteeds."

"And the gear to ride them," Zu added.

"Yeah. Figure out what we absolutely can't live without, and put it in a pile, and we'll trade the rest. But don't make it obvious there are two piles, or we might as well just hand them everything."

Alan looked at Karjan. "Can you trade what's in your pack?"

Karjan looked alarmed. "No, I cannot. It is personal."

"We might need every possible item to trade. You have to have something in there," Alan said as he reached for the bag.

Karjan jerked away. "You would not understand. It is personal, and I cannot leave it."

Alan sighed. "Okay, find some other stuff to get rid of. I'll be back."

* * *

The children signed for Alan to a set of stunned adults whom Alan could only assume were leaders — or in charge of the Heliosteeds. Alan signed he wanted to trade, but the leaders refused the idea of parting with Heliosteeds.

This is going to be difficult.

Alan showed a set of flashlights, fire starters, and other tools. The leaders expressed timid interest in the lights but still refused.

He returned to the group of men.

"I'm having trouble. Have you figured out things to offer?" Alan asked.

Mup hoisted the bag onto his back. "Let me deal with them. Remember, I'm the one who got the artifact to begin with."

"Combs," Alan said.

"Combs," Mup repeated.

"Please tell me we are offering more than combs," Zu said.

"I can't promise," Mup said, "but if they like combs so much, who am I to judge? Three Heliosteeds, right?"

"Three. And gear for five riders," Alan said. "And help to get the gear on the birds."

Tier and Karjan glanced at each other.

"Be back in a moon's split." Mup disappeared into the rain.

A wild wind whipped in from the jungle and spread through the village, eliciting wild chitters and more drumming.

* * *

A group of well-groomed Heliops helped carry the men's belongings through the rain to the Heliosteed enclosures. Behind them, the men followed, who themselves were trailed by a troop of Heliop children carrying bundles of leather gear.

The adults led the group to a set of enclosures that held three large, soaking-wet Heliosteeds. One of the adult Heliops pointed to three enclosures, and a child signed: Man. Heliosteed.

Alan walked to his enclosure and opened the door. The Heliosteed inside was dimly illuminated. Massive leaves had been fixed to the paddock to keep out rain, but the attempt was in vain. The Heliosteed's body was a shimmering, wet shadow. It huffed and shuffled nervously. A child shoved half a large fruit in Alan's hands. Alan approached the beast with a false confidence, hoping the perceptive creature would not detect it.

A far-off flash of lightning briefly revealed the creature's details. It was a tremendous bird, its eyes piercing and reptilian.

Alan held the fruit up so the bird could smell it. The bird croaked cautiously, and Alan lobbed the fruit into the air and heard the bird catching it and crushing it into bits with its long beak.

The child Heliop gently pushed Alan, urging him to move to the beast and touch it. Alan closed his eyes and recalled how Green had walked along the bird, dragging a hand through its feathers and showing it his intentions.

Together, the child and Alan set about laying out the leather harness and bridle in the dark. The child was quick but patient with Alan as they fumbled through the work.

Soon, the bird was rigged for flight.

The young Heliop grabbed Alan's arm and guided him out of the enclosure, then led him to where the other men and adults had gathered. Alan recognized many of the adult Heliops from the flight earlier in the day. Alan saw Green and signed a greeting.

The child that had helped Alan chittered to Green, who responded in kind.

The child signed: Heliops. Fly. Men. Fly. Ceto.

Pausing for a moment, the child then mimed what Alan could only interpret as a new sign for *together*.

Alan replied: Yes.

As the child turned to speak to Green, Alan grabbed his shoulder and signed: Fly. Rain. Question.

Understanding the question, the child nodded — which in Heliop culture meant "no."

No flying in the rain. Good, it's already dark.

"Alan," Mup called, "when are we leaving? Now?"

"I don't think so. Not during the rain, at least," Alan replied.

"It'll be impossible to see anything," Zu added. "How are we supposed to follow them?"

"Aren't we just going straight up?" Mup asked.

"There has to be something more," Alan said.

The young Heliop interrupted: Man. Heliop. Eat. Rain. No.

* * *

The interior of the Heliop home was spacious, single-roomed, and well kept—clearly, a lodging that had been maintained over many generations. Despite the pummeling rains and violent winds, the low profile of the home kept the occupants dry.

The lodge, however, was smoky and filled with smells familiar only to the Heliops.

The home was communal. Around most of the edge of the circular lodge were nests of branches and leaves covered with animal skins. To Alan, each nest appeared to be an individual's bed. Near the beds, attached to the lattice of branches and wood that made up the walls of the home, were decorations from many materials. He recognized many that appeared to be at least partially constructed from shards of artifact metals.

On the far end of the lodge, away from the leather-draped door, was a set of nests in which a few white-haired Heliops lay sleeping, curled into tight balls.

Great leather sheets hung from the ceiling, decorations imprinted and colored to show scenes of Heliops flying, dancing, and cooking. Alan had noticed the Heliops did not seem to have any artwork that alluded to battles between the creatures—only scenes from daily life.

Away from the edges of the walkway, Heliops corralled their belongings in long, fenced areas. Within the fences were communal piles of leather belts and household tools.

At the center of the home was an ever-burning fire over which a stand had been built for cooking.

Around the central fire, the men and Heliops squatted in the pit that allowed the home to have lofty ceilings but not be exposed to the winds. The Heliops spoke to each other in soft tones and whistles, their ears stiller than Alan had seen before. Alan realized that those in the pit were all riders, aside from one child that stuck close to the men to translate.

Heliops of all varieties brought in foods and placed them in the center near the fire. Alan recognized some dishes: fruit he had enjoyed immensely, the eyeballs he had not, meat that reminded him of pig, and more meat that reminded him of sand. One of the feasts, a bug the size of Alan's hand, took to its feet and trudged away with its many legs.

The men waited for the Heliops. When the last dish was placed in the center, the Heliop riders shuffled in and began picking food to eat. The group left little room for the men.

"Elbow in," Mup said.

He's probably right, Alan thought as he forcefully pushed aside two Heliops. *I hope there is still some fruit.*

Tightly pressed, shoulder to shoulder, the group ate greedily. Alan wondered if this was a custom meant to show appreciation for the food that had been provided.

"Alan," Zu started with a mouth half full, "can you say you've had a more fulfilling day? First—" Zu stopped, startled as his furry neighbor took fruit from his hands. "Blast it! He took my fruit!"

The men laughed, and the Heliops looked on, their ears quivering in approval.

Zu pointedly took a piece of the meat sand from the dish in front of his neighbor and made an exhibition of eating it noisily while staring at the thief.

"I was saying," Zu continued, looking at Alan, "first, we are taught by these wonderful creatures how to fly other wonderful creatures. We have lunch with a view—"

"Escape a flying monster," Alan added.

"*Blast* a flying monster," Mup corrected.

"Find out we aren't going to die," Zu continued.

"But instead find out we will get a front-row seat to the most amazing event in the galaxy," Mup said.

"Not just a front-row seat," Alan said, looking to Mup. "We will be a part of the most amazing event in the galaxy."

The men were quiet.

"Here is to the most amazing event in the galaxy," Alan said, holding up a limp chunk of fleshy fruit.

"Here is to the most amazing event in the galaxy," Mup repeated, holding up his own dish.

"Cheers," Zu said. "And to us. That this is the start of many more amazing adventures together."

"Well said!" Mup exclaimed.

"Many more," Tier and Karjan added together.

Alan realized the Heliops were staring at the men, unfamiliar with their strange custom. "And to the Heliops, though they don't know it!"

The men laughed and the entire group resumed the messy ordeal of eating.

As the food continued to disappear, Mup sat up from the meal before him.

"The rain… it's stopped."

The other men paused their eating.

The Heliops noticed the men had stopped eating and also paused. Looking toward the ceiling of the home, the Heliops ears scanned side to side, listening for the sounds of the storm.

"Indeed, it has," Zu said.

"And the music…" Mup said.

The young Heliop next to Alan looked at the men, the fire casting playful shadows on his face.

The child signed: Fly.

Chapter 14
Ceto

T he group emerged from the lodge to a sea of silence and an atmosphere of stillness. Around the building, the Heliop village had congregated and stood along the path to the paddocks to watch the riders as they made their way to the Heliosteeds. A Heliop bystander occasionally reached out and touched one of the riders; the rider reacted with lowered ears and continued walking.

Do they ever see their family again? Alan wondered.

The riders passed the gate to the paddock, and the village moved to follow. The crowds gathered at the small fence to watch quietly as the riders opened their enclosures and made their way in to join their Heliosteeds and young assistants.

Alan entered the enclosure and strapped on his backpack. He brought the straps over his shoulders and clasped a set of cords across his chest. He pulled the shoulder straps tight. His assistant attached the riding belt snugly above his hips and stood back.

Alan looked at the bird and then to the other Heliop riders.

Yet, the riders did not mount. The men saw the riders were standing by their mounts quietly, so they followed and waited patiently.

A break in the clouds and a tremendous shaft of aurora light shone down—a beam of many colors that illuminated the village in twinkling and dancing patterns. Then, an incredible flash as veins of lightning crawled across the sky a hundred thousand feet above. As the lightning moved, it turned from blue to green to yellow and back to blue. It strobed briefly and disappeared. He was unsure if the lightning had burned itself into his eyes or if the phenomenon took time to dissipate.

A line of Heliops appeared on the path, walking toward the enclosures, each Heliop carrying a thick, long, wooden vessel that appeared to be holding liquid. The line of Heliops dispersed into pairs at each enclosure, including the men's, and walked in. They stopped in front of each rider.

In silence, each rider lowered himself to a squat. The men followed, gently urged by their young attendant.

Alan knelt, looking at the ground. A Heliop stood behind him, and suddenly he felt a cold slime slap against his back, then his shoulders and hair. The Heliop was throwing handfuls of muck across him. It paused for a moment to put its vessel on the ground, then rubbed the mess all over Alan's body.

The smell! Alan thought as his nose filled with the scent of... flowers.

The Heliop paused, and Alan heard him pick up the vessel and walk to the Heliosteed. The assistant lowered the bird into a prone position, and the sound of glop falling on the bird's wings alerted Alan that the bird was suffering the same fate. He waited as the Heliop finished spreading the ooze all over the bird, the sounds of hollow wood revealing that all the liquid had been spent.

The two came back to stand near Alan, then took up a position beside the kneeling man. He waited, assuming the other enclosures had not finished the ritual.

A distant whistle sounded, and the second Heliop moved toward Alan. He reached into his vessel, withdrew, and blew into his hand, spreading a dust across Alan.

Sparkles of light caught Alan's periphery, blue pinpricks igniting on his clothes, and suddenly a blast of light as the dust settled all over his body. He felt no sensation beyond wonder as the gel all over him lit up into a brilliant blaze of blue glowing aura. He stood, looking at his body, moving his arms.

"Amazing!" he whispered to himself.

The glow of his body illuminated the enclosure as if he were a brilliant torch. Heliops looked on, their bodies awash in the blue tint from Alan's glow. The Heliosteed watched as well from its prone position, a sheen of the oily substance covering it. All the other enclosures radiated light — each shining brightly, and crowds of Heliops stood nearby, transfixed.

The second Heliop took his vessel to the Heliosteed and blew the dust. As it landed, the Heliosteed lit up in a shining blaze. The Heliop circled the bird, blowing dust over its wings and body. The birds cast a dull blue light on the broken clouds passing by above.

A wind, a gust, rippled through the village, breaking the stillness. The lodges creaked, and the leather awnings flapped noisily before going quiet. The crowd of onlookers shuffled. A second gust came through, lighter than the first.

Alan heard Heliops mounting their birds. He looked to his assistant then walked to his own bird.

Time to prove what I'm made of, he thought to himself as his heartbeat pounded in his ears. He approached the bird like the Heliops had taught him and moved his hand along its head, over its neck, and along its shoulders. He climbed onto the bird and threw his leg over its body so he straddled its back.

The glowing creature and rider joined.

The bird breathed in deeply and exhaled noisily as if it knew a tremendous journey was imminent.

Alan quickly tied himself to the bird and attached the reins to his belt. He felt around the bird's body with his feet and found loops to secure himself into—the stirrups that were uncomfortable now but necessary for when the bird stood. The assistant walked around the Heliosteed, checking each strap, pulling and twisting to make sure they were secure. Alan did his own checks—once, twice, and a third time.

Better to know now that every strap is perfect and secure rather than find out in flight. Last thing I want to worry about—a loose strap.

He sat anxiously, adjusting his sitting. *Come on, what are we waiting for?*

Another gust blew through the village, this time knocking over something that had not been stored. It rolled noisily behind the onlookers and fell into a pit. The enclosures creaked as the gust blew and then subsided. Another gust, this one tremendous and violent. He was stunned as he felt flying dust and debris blast his face. He put his head close to the bird to protect himself.

The blast did not relent, and he thought he heard the top of the enclosure rip open. He looked up and saw the glowing lattice of the ceiling missing, drawn back by the wind or a Heliop.

Here we go!

A loud whistle Alan recognized blasted, and the bird shot up to its feet and threw itself into the air with a tremendous thrust of energy. Like a rocket, the bird and rider flew into a massive current of a violent wind.

Barely past the enclosure, he saw the rising lights of the many Heliosteeds, lit up like brilliant blue flares, rising into the surrounding sky. Four to his left, four to his right—each bird flapping and tumbling in the violent winds, the rider visible as a blob of blue on top of their mount.

Alan knew that to his left were all Heliops and to his right men, so he pulled his mount to turn and head toward the riders to his left. The bird struggled to keep a course in the wind but quickly found itself following a climbing set of Heliosteeds. He looked back and saw that the riders behind had also turned to join the train of voyagers.

With the wind to their back, he felt an incredible sense of speed, as if the bird were not flying as much as being taken along for a ride in the storm. The bird continued to thrust its wings, trying to keep altitude with those it followed.

They rose quickly, flying to what he could only guess was a few thousand feet. They had been blown far away from the village and back under a layer of cloud. The sky gone, everything around them disappeared into a pitch-black void — only the other birds providing any reference.

They flew, the winds hurtling them along into the darkness. A deep fear shot through him that it was impossible to navigate and that no one could know where they were going with nothing to guide them.

Without warning, a cold, violent blast of air fell upon the train, and he could see all the birds tumble and scatter as if an explosion had knocked them in all directions. He felt his bird rolling in the wind, unable to keep level flight. Suddenly, everything around the two lit up — they had fallen into the clouds. Disorientation took over, and he saw only the blinding light of himself and his bird in a sea of glowing blue mist. Every direction was the reflected light of the bird and rider — like a torch in fog. Then they quickly shot out of the haze — a light not his own, a glimmer of the sky, and it disappeared again. Back into the clouds. Neither the bird nor Alan could tell what orientation they were in. Were they diving to their death or flying upward in a vertical pitch?

Dead already.

The bird flapped its wings, feeling to him like it had panicked, unable to tell where it was heading.

Then, a glowing haze not their own appeared and rolled away.

The Heliosteed fixed itself on the glow and stopped its tumble. The glow stopped moving, and the Heliosteed found the familiar rush of air that pushed against their back. With forceful thrusts, the bird urged on toward the light, which cleared into the outline of another Heliosteed.

Alan's Heliosteed followed the lone bird, and he quietly hoped that the creature ahead could itself see others in front of it.

He glanced over his left shoulder and then his right — *there!* Another Heliosteed was trailing them in the distance.

If we don't get lost in these clouds, there is hope.

The trio of birds turned into six before the next air current pushed up from underneath. The train of flyers lifted dramatically higher. At the front of the pack, the lead weaved back and forth shallowly, sensing the boundaries of the lift.

As suddenly as they had found themselves within the haze of deep clouds, they emerged, exposed to a sudden brilliant landscape of wild auroras and constant pulses of lightning showering roiling cloud tops with green and purple light. The clouds themselves occasionally sparkled into wild blooms of color from the lightning within.

He realized they were in a tremendous column of clear air, wider than the crater valley: the eye of the storm. The air was pushing them up and forward with less turbulence, as if they were riding in a giant whirlpool. Only the sound of air rushing through the features of his mount and through his ears. Around them, the walls of the storm reached tens of thousands of feet up before being pulled into long strands of brilliant haze that reached into the auroras and out to meet the storm of Ceto. The auroras, he realized, were the demarcation between the two planets — where the energy of the two planets' atmospheres brushing along each other transformed into a spectacle of lightning and color.

The nearest wall was a few miles to the northwest from where the group flew. The leader of the train quickly aimed the group toward it.

As they floated higher above the cloud ceilings, Alan scanned behind and below for the missing riders. Then, as if sensing how far behind they were, three Heliosteeds appeared from the clouds, like fireflies caught in the wind.

He breathed relief and looked across the storm eye. In the far distance, miles away, he thought he could make out another train of lights — a string of what looked like twenty green embers flying slowly upward.

He looked up. *Still so much to go.* Then he leaned over and looked down. A fall now and he would never be seen again. He felt a sudden sense of vertigo and lowered himself slightly against the steadiness of the Heliosteed.

The wall ahead grew in size.

He could see the strategy now. The walls of the storm were tremendous bastions of upward energy, and the leader hoped to use them as an elevator upward to Ceto. By staying near the edge of the wall, the light from the auroras could be used as orientation.

But the price of the ride was going to be a violent thrashing.

Stay close to the others, but if you get separated, weave out, orient, and go back in, riding up.

The wind to their backs, the small group of riders worked toward the wall. As they got closer, the winds became turbulent and chaotic—sometimes lifting them dramatically, only to reverse and push them down. The chain of birds transformed from a straight line, arrowing toward the walls of the storm, into an undulating form trying to stay together.

Every passing moment, Alan thought they must be at the point of entry into the wall of clouds—but still, the ride continued. He looked up, his eyes following the storm walls until it felt as if the vapors were looming *over* and behind him. The light of the aurora played on the wall as if it were a tumult of colored lightning within.

Another sudden lift, dramatic and powerful. He lowered his gaze to focus on the riders in front of him and saw they were illuminating veils of cloud as they passed through them. Subtle, at first, a bit of cloud only revealed by the passing glow of a rider and then suddenly and completely—each bird disappearing into a blue haze. He watched the bird in front of him disappear, and then he found himself in a mist of blue light, surrounded by an endless sea of thick clouds whipping by.

Calm. Stay calm.

Alan and the Heliosteed both froze, balancing in the brightness, letting the tremendous updrafts push them higher.

The clouds broke momentarily, and he glimpsed the others, scattered but still heading in the same direction. They disappeared individually, and soon he was in another thick realm of clouds whipping by.

To his right, he could see the flashing, changing colors of the auroras. He nudged the Heliosteed, and it carefully glided toward the edge of the wall before emerging back into the eye.

As they cleared out into the center of the storm, the strong uplift turned back into turbulent vortices of shearing winds.

Quickly, Alan surveyed his position as the Heliosteed tried to keep a straight flight. Above and ahead a mile, a glowing Heliosteed skirted with the edge of the wall and disappeared. Behind, far behind, another Heliosteed emerged and loitered into the clear of the eye. The group was laddering up the storm—riding the uplifts and popping out to orient before moving back in.

He looked down to the floor of the storm and gasped at the incredible height they had gained. Looking up, he could see that the auroras were getting closer.

Gaping up into the storm's eye, into the aurora, he thought for a moment that he saw tiny flecks of light falling from above. He scanned and then caught them again: a train of pink lights falling out of the aurora towards Helios. He continued focusing, unsure if what he was seeing was real or not, and realized the specks were growing and getting closer. Then, he recognized the tiny lights for what they were: illuminated Heliosteeds migrating from the ocean planet to the jungles of Helios. As he tracked them, he realized they were approaching with great velocity through the center of the storm. Within a few seconds, they were rocketing by in a vertical dive far off to his right. In his mind, he wished the travelers well on their journey.

Leaning to his left, Alan urged the Heliosteed back into the wall of the storm—back into the strong updrafts. As they entered the blinding glow of the cloud wall, the lift of the storm pushed the Heliosteed up and forced him to lay his chest against the bird. Upward they traveled.

Alan and his bird had begun to understand the rhythm of climbing the storm—the alternating steps of riding the storm and emerging to orient, each requiring a different style of flying. Within the storm, the Heliosteed focused on staying stable and letting the moody lift push them upward—not using his wings for thrust but gliding and riding each column efficiently. When the pair emerged from the storm, the Heliosteed struggled mightily to navigate the opposing winds of the interior and avoid losing control and falling into a tumbling vortex.

Each repeated sequence of moving in and out of the storm wall brought him and the other riders higher into the sky—the air becoming cooler and cooler.

The wall of clouds had turned gradually thinner, less dramatic, and filled with the diffused light of the aurora. Buffeting winds had transformed into a steady current of air, and the Heliosteed relaxed. The bird rocked itself gently, as if standing on a balancing beam, riding the air without tipping. The columns of air had settled into a uniform but strong lift. The winds of a storm transformed into a jet of air pushing out into space.

He could see farther now. From within the thinner storm walls, he saw a thousand feet in every direction, as if floating on a river moving through a nebula. Ahead and behind, above and below, the scattered Heliosteeds and their riders were visible—all riding the same energy upward. Alan counted and found all the riders who had left the village.

Higher and higher they drifted.

The auroras had once been clean, sharp curtains of light, whipping through the sky like a piece of silk caught in a breeze. Now, he realized, he couldn't make out their edges—only that the changing colors of them were all around. They had entered the domain of the auroras.

It was a dreamscape of beating lights, vibrant colors, and streaming rivers of haze. He had never seen or heard anything described like what he was now seeing — *living.*

The gravity — it's neutralizing.

As he sensed his own weight falling away, the Heliosteed tilted erratically, as if confused by the sense of falling while every other sense showed flying.

Calm, calm, he thought as he urged the creature to steady itself.

The feeling of climbing upward had gradually relented to the sensation of falling forward. Up was straight, down was behind.

The bird remained unsure, wavering its wings and turning its head side to side to make sense of the creeping feeling. He laid his body against the bird and held his hands to its side.

Calm, calm.

The bird settled, its jerking catches slowing in frequency. Together the pair found themselves floating gently in the serene cavern of clouds, undulations of aurora light playing and settling on the pair. The Heliosteed flapped gently to continue following the other birds that glowed far ahead.

Alan realized, as he pushed his body against the warm bird, that he had become cold. The column of warm jungle air that the duo had drafted on had dissipated, but enough heat had funneled up from Helios to the high altitudes to keep Alan and his bird from quickly freezing to death.

Out of the corner of his eye, off the right wing of the bird, Alan caught a dim whip of light flash by. A moment later, another flying light zipped over — too fast to make sense of it.

He sat up and squinted into the distance ahead —

Rain? Snow?

A cloud of tiny specks, droplets of some kind, was appearing ahead. The leaders continued onward into the haze.

One of the grains of light in the haze grew suddenly and splashed into Alan's face as if he were staring up into the rain.

Water.

More thick droplets smacked against him and the bird. The droplets were larger than rain, the size of small stones. He leaned forward into his bird and made himself small.

The Heliosteed was having to beat its wings to keep up with the other birds. The free ride up was over, and the calm air of the auroras needed to be pulled through.

More water hit his head, then his shoulders. Suddenly, he was hit by something that lodged between himself and the bird. The object was hard and soft at the same time, but also moving with the wind.

He grabbed the thing quickly, reactively, and was about to toss it when he realized it felt familiar in his hands.

A small twig with leaves.

He looked at it, unbelieving, only to be hit by another twig and a quick storm of leaves. He raised his head and saw the haze ahead was a cloud of debris floating in the aurora.

The Heliosteed's head jerked back as a larger branch of leaves caught around the bird's beak. Annoyed, the creature shook its head quickly until the branch broke free and tumbled over the Heliosteed's back and into Alan before falling away.

The rain of debris continued, colliding with the bird and hitting Alan even as he hid his face in the bird's back.

Then came a solid smack to the shoulder, a blast like a rock that sent pain down his arm. He grabbed his shoulder; it felt cold.

The Heliosteed continued flying and suddenly dodged to the left and came back to center. Alan lifted his head cautiously. A gnarled spheroid of ice whizzed by fifty feet from the Heliosteed's right wing.

A few hundred feet ahead, the group of Heliosteeds cautiously navigated the debris field. A thousand feet ahead of them, enormous clumps of ice loitered.

Alan gripped the reins and urged the Heliosteed to sprint to catch up with the group.

It'll be easier to fly this course close on the tail of another rider. Just don't get killed by a stray chunk of something.

The Heliosteed obeyed Alan's pressings but juked left and right to dodge debris at its own will. Without warning, a shapeless glob flew past the Heliosteed's head, hit Alan directly in the chest, and splashed his neck and arms with icy water.

Close call.

Flapping its wings furiously, the Heliosteed weaved past clumps of branches, streaks of water, and occasional balls of ice tumbling through the air. They arrived at the tail of the pack of birds, who themselves had formed a compact line.

He checked his rear and was surprised to find a trail of four birds.

Everyone has the same idea.

Ahead, the field of ice rocks loomed, denser, and more formidable than he had realized.

The leader of the train broke right, and every bird behind followed the lead, peeling away as a man-sized chunk of ice flew by beneath them. They flew over a smaller cluster of ice, then underneath a tumbling boulder.

A glimmering chunk of ice moved across their train's line of flight and collided with another equally massive rock, and with a deep crackle and explosion, shards flew out in every direction. Disaster.

The Heliosteeds scattered under, over, and around the hailstorm. Alan shielded his face, but neither he nor his Heliosteed escaped the punishment of shards big and small slashing at them and falling away. As they tumbled through the shower, ice continued to strike from every direction, pelting the bird and rider. As they escaped, he realized the group had dispersed and was trying to move back together, but obstacles from every direction complicated the task.

A bird nearby was reachable, and Alan guided his own ride to group up. Just a hundred feet ahead...

A tremendous block of ice was moving down from above — imposing and unwavering. The lead rider looked up to gauge its path while pushing his bird into a shallow dive to curl underneath it. An oblong ice boulder, sharp-edged and tumbling wildly, shot up from underneath — in the blind spot of the rider. Alan shouted in vain and instinctively put his Heliosteed into an evasive right bank.

Over his shoulder, he watched as the tumbling ice boulder crashed into the lead Heliosteed, sending it shooting upward in an uncontrolled mass into the mammoth ice rock above. The dead Heliosteed slammed against the rock, instantly killing its rider.

Have to get through this!

His Heliosteed skimmed along the surface of an iceberg and darted across a gap to another.

At least I only have to watch what's above me.

Ahead, he saw a pair of Heliosteeds moving perpendicular to his path. The Heliosteed knew from instinct to form up with the pair and maneuvered from rock to rock, weaving madly to avoid stray ice.

Rider and bird curled into a tight bank over and around the top of an ice boulder and found the pair of Heliosteeds ahead. Diving like a bird of prey, the creature swooped in behind and joined the formation of riders. He could see that both birds had two riders: Mup, Zu, Karjan, and Tier.

"Mup!" Alan shouted.

The group turned around to see Alan following close behind.

"Good to see you, Alan! This is horrible flying!" Mup replied. "Take the lead; you have to be more maneuverable. We'll follow!"

Alan acknowledged by urging his bird into a sprint to take the lead as it moved into a long, left bank to avoid a cluster of ice boulders. Keeping up an intense pace, he broke his lead to a hundred feet — enough to give the others time to react to his maneuvers.

The floating chunks of ice had gotten thicker but, as a result, were moving slower and more predictably. His Heliosteed confidently flew over the ice, skimming the surface and moving from rock to rock, the others following behind.

Suddenly, the ice let up, and before them was a large group of Heliosteeds and their riders. They had found the group on the other side. Before them were clouds of debris with stray ice chunks falling away from the band of ice rocks. Beyond the debris, colored strands of cloud reached out to a great storm ahead – below. They were now looking down into Ceto from within the misty auroras far above its surface. To his right, far in the distance, was an explosion of light over a crescent of darkness – dawn.

Just have to navigate these last challenges – straight down to Ceto!

The debris field was no less brutal than the first one the riders had encountered. All matter of debris loosened up from the jungle by colossal storms now lingered high above the surface, pelting the riders mercilessly.

Suddenly, a slap and a sharp pain hit Alan's right arm – the pain so sudden and fierce he could only clench his teeth. He grabbed at his arm and felt a sharp splinter of metal sticking out of his bicep. Without thinking, he quickly pulled out the object and pinched it between his fingers. He knew before looking at it what it was – a tiny shard of blue and red metal.

Blasted piece of…! Of all the things to get stabbed by!

He felt around clumsily for a pocket and stuffed the memento into his jacket.

If I'm getting stabbed and pummeled, this poor bird is going to be dead on arrival!

As he focused on stopping the bleeding of his arm, he recognized a familiar sensation returning – falling.

Gradually the Heliosteed stopped flapping as it picked up speed naturally in a glide. Faster and faster, they moved through the debris – leaves becoming stinging reminders of what a storm could pick up.

As the speed increased, Alan sensed the Heliosteed converting its body into an arrow, curling its wings into its frame for a dive. The cold wind whipped over the bird's back and pummeled Alan, pulled at his hair, and blasted his ears. The group far ahead was moving away. He leaned into the bird once more and sneaked a glance at the followers. Behind, the other Heliosteed's profiles looked like enormous seabirds diving to water.

The debris disappeared, and the group moved along at incredible speeds, following long bands of gentle clouds toward the dense mass of storm. The rising star cast long shadows on the surface of the planet, the high reaches of the Ceto storm casting a dark shade on the surface directly below them.

If the walls of the storm are the updraft – then the center of the storm must be the downdraft. Aim for that and go all the way to the surface.

The group passed over the walls of the Ceto storm and plunged down into the dark eye – shielded from the light of the morning sun. The column of clouds now loomed above and behind, the sunlight disappearing suddenly, the air beginning to thicken and warm.

Then, without warning, he felt his Heliosteed extend its wings and arrest the dive. The weight of multiple gravities pulled at him as the dive turned into a glide.

He sat up, suddenly aware of the lack of wind blasting at him, trying to rip him away from the back of the bird. Gliding felt serene, stable – silent.

Around him, he counted the other riders. He was relieved to see only one had been lost in the passing, and he wondered if the others had noticed the absence. The Heliops surely would notice, but without a translator, he could not comfort them – telling them the death was quick and unforeseen.

The group formed a long snake in the sky, lazily making circles so broad they could hardly be perceived, lowering themselves gradually into the calm of the eye.

Above, the sky had become a steady, brilliant pink and was starting to shift to blue. The walls of the clouds reflected the light, and the interior of the eye glowed in the morning sun. Below the riders were scattered clouds, and below that, dark black oceans.

Alan watched the landscape below, as did the other riders. The journey's ultimate disaster of nowhere to land would be realized without sight of an island — and with this thought, the wisdom of breaking into a glide at a high altitude became clear to him.

As he circled slowly towards the surface of the planet, he realized that the blue gel that covered his skin and illuminated the journey had dried into dust. The light it had provided was now extinguished and the sandy remains blew away in the breeze of flight.

Suddenly, a whistle sounded from one of the Heliosteeds, and a rider broke from the line and entered a dive off to the left. The other birds, one by one, broke away and followed the plunge.

Alan looked at Mup and Zu, waved, and followed the other Heliops into the dive.

Ahead, on the surface of the ink-black ocean was a long, green jewel of an island with a single towering mountain. Surrounding the green land was a long, thick ring of tan-and-white beaches — far more than he would have expected.

The planets' encounter — it's pulling the ocean away from the island. An enormous outgoing tide.

As the group angled its dive, the central mountain revealed the far side of the island. Lying close to shore on the exposed ocean floor was the unmistakable profile of an enormous spacecraft — hundreds of yards long, resting in two pieces, partially buried.

There it is.

Chapter 15
Seed

The sun peeked over the far edge of the storm, and beams of light reached the forested island in the center of the dark ocean. The line of Heliosteeds, a thousand feet over the water, approached the shores.

It was clear as the group approached that the ocean had receded magnitudes farther than normal. The shoreline extended thousands of feet away from the island, great forests of kelp flattened, giving way to deeper slopes covered in sea creatures unaccustomed to being exposed to the atmosphere. Hundreds of pools where water had become trapped dotted the landscape — some of them draining in through a myriad of tiny waterfalls.

The Heliops headed directly for the nearest edge of the forest. Alan realized it was time to part ways and set out for the other side of the island, where the wrecked ship lay.

Alan whooped loudly and waved his hand as he broke rank. The Heliops riders turned to look and saw Alan and the other men veer off to follow the shore. Cautiously, the lead rider mimicked Alan's wave in return and set back to flying to the forest.

Not much for goodbyes.

Alan's eyes followed the Heliops' glide path and saw clusters of figures appearing from the forest onto the shores.

The landscape of the island was completely different from Helios. The air was cool, thick, and perfumed with the scent of the ocean. The forest was made of thick groves of what looked to be pine trees — completely lacking broadleaf siblings of any kind. At the center of the island was a jagged crag of splintered rock shooting up so steeply that near its peaks only the hardiest of foliage found refuge in protected nooks. The mountain itself now towered above the riders, who slowly descended the last few hundred feet.

Past the mountain, in Alan's line of sight, was the distant wall of the storm.

A hundred miles away, but not much more. The far wall will be here in two hours' time. A complication — not a lot of time to make sense of the wreck and explore.

The wreck came into view from behind the foothills of the mountain. The vessel was massive, as large as the cargo ships Alan had seen at the space stations above the Core systems.

Shaped like a flattened cylinder, the ship was broken in the center and half-submerged into ocean floor sediment. The near end of the wreckage barely reached the edge of the forest, surprising Alan.

That part must always be exposed. Not impossible to find from above, but also not obvious unless you were looking.

The color and texture of the skin of the wreckage clearly demarcated the portions of the ship that were usually submerged. Changing color from the signature reddish-blue tint, the crumpled, exposed end of the ship was a rough skin of green and brown layers of organic material. The ocean had long made a home out of most of the wreck.

Water streamed out of holes in the vessel creating white, arcing waterfalls.

"There it is!" Zu shouted from his Heliosteed nearby. "That has to be the origin!"

"It certainly is!" Alan replied.

Tier and Karjan, riding on separate birds with Mup and Zu, leaned out to gawk at the ship.

"It looks like we don't have a lot of time," Mup shouted as he pointed to the distant wall of clouds. "That'll be here in an hour or two. It's our ride back unless you want to live here!"

"We'll survey the wreck from above, figure out how to best use our time, and go in," Alan replied, miming a circling bird with his hand.

"Good plan!" Zu shouted.

Alan and the others moved closer to the wreck, its scale becoming clearer as they approached.

This would take dozens of years to make sense of, Alan thought as he scanned the vessel with his eyes. *Every foot of this thing is invaluable.*

The vessel's long, relatively smooth uniform shape was interrupted by a blistering protrusion on the second half of the ship farthest from the shore. Alan navigated closer and entered a low orbit to investigate its details.

He could not find any ports, hatches, or windows on the blister. Yet, the feature clearly had importance to the whole of the ship — its unique structure and position making it of either engineering or cultural significance.

"This. This is where we will start." Alan pointed to the bulbous feature. "I don't know what it is, but it must serve some important purpose."

"It's where I'd put sensors or command crew," Mup called, "or both."

Alan and the others brought their Heliosteeds to a landing on the feature. Up close, the surface of the vessel was a wet mess of sea plants and strange creatures that made the wreckage their home.

"The inside is going to be a mess," Mup said as he unstrapped his belt.

"And it's going to be dark," Alan said. "I wish we had more of that luminescent goo the Heliops smeared all over us."

Tier and Karjan were both the first off the Heliosteeds. "I thought that ride would never end," Karjan complained.

Alan swung himself off his Heliosteed and landed unsteadily on the surface of the wreck, his boots crunching on shelled creatures.

"I would say that flight was both the best and worst experience of my life. I wish I didn't know we had to turn around and do it again," Alan said to Karjan.

"I feel for the Heliosteed," Karjan replied.

The Heliosteed! Alan turned to look at the bird.

The bird's face had clearly taken a beating, but its hard beak and leathered skin had survived without major injury. Alan had never appreciated how durable the creature was — as if it had been bred for the task of flying a gauntlet of ice and forest debris.

"I'm surprised it survived," Alan said with wonder.

"Mine didn't seem very happy," Mup replied.

Zu landed on the ship and slipped immediately, catching himself on his Heliosteed. The bird watched Zu cautiously with one eye.

"Get the equipment off the birds, and let's give them a break and get inside," Alan said to the group.

Tier and Karjan began unstrapping the bags that had been saddled on Zu and Mup's birds.

"I figure we can either bust in through the top, maybe over there," — Mup pointed to a lump in the skin — "or we can work our way into a break over there where I saw a waterfall."

"Seed metal is brittle most of the time but takes some effort to make the first breaks. A hot cutter will work well," Alan said.

"You have a hot cutter?" Mup asked.

"Of course. Why else would I bring it up?" Alan replied as he unstrapped his backpack.

"I don't know, just thought you liked talking about Seed metal."

"I always like talking about Seed metal," Alan said as he produced a small, hooked metal tool, "but I don't talk just to talk."

Alan twisted an end of the tool, and the opposite end glowed bright blue. He touched the glow to an exposed portion of wreckage skin, which sparked lightly and melted, but as he reached the sea life that had attached to the vessel, the creatures exploded and shot bits of flesh and carapace all over Alan. He switched off the tool and rubbed at an eye he held shut.

"Okay, we'll need to get this stuff off of where we want to cut. This is a job for you guys," Alan said.

After the sea life had been scrubbed off, Alan continued. The first layer of cutting allowed him into a secondary hull, filled with conduits and honeycomb materials — clearly not an inhabitable space. He continued cutting into the floor to reach the next space. With a quick set of lines etched into the flooring of the second hull, he was able to stomp the floor out and into the third hull space.

Alan hung his body down into the empty area, shining his flashlight into the void below. It was a room, small and wet, encrusted with ocean growth. At a glance, this *was* a room used by the spacefarers. The floor was far down, twelve feet, but some loose materials nearby could be stacked to use as a ladder to escape.

The Seed were tall.

"All right, I cut into the habitable areas!" Alan called up the column he had cut. Mup, standing watch from above, repeated Alan's findings, then sat at the edge of the hole and started climbing down.

Alan dropped into the room with a splash and a slight stumble. The room had trapped a knee-deep pool of seawater. Under his feet, Alan could feel the crunching of ocean debris. A warm pungent smell of brine and seaweed filled the room — a reminder that the spacefaring ship was now serving as a reef in an ocean. He turned on his flashlight and scanned the room. Tiny sea creatures that had made the space their home recoiled into the shadows as light cast across them. Anything not made of Seed metal had long since decayed, leaving only blocks of oddly shaped equipment and long rods piled on one side of the room, all covered in alien growth.

He grabbed a tall, metal box covered in mud and sand and shoved it into position underneath the entrance hole. Grabbing some of the miscellaneous rods, Alan reinforced the box upright. As soon as it was all in place, Mup dropped down and splashed into the water.

Tier and Karjan climbed down the column one after another and stopped above the entrance to the room.

"Karjan, go first. I'll pass my pack down to you," Tier said.

"I can get it," Mup interrupted, looking up the hole.

"Thank you, but Karjan and I will handle it," Tier replied curtly.

"No, really, I insist," Mup continued.

Karjan ignored Mup and removed his pack, handed it to Tier, and dropped down. Tier lowered Karjan's pack, which Karjan put on, then lowered his own pack, which Karjan held on to until Tier lowered himself. The two moved off the stand and onto the floor as Zu clambered down the hole.

"What is this place?" Karjan asked.

"I don't know, but it's not what we're looking for," Alan replied.

"How will we know what we're looking for?" Mup asked.

"I think we'll know. We want to find a bridge with anything related to navigation. Or," Alan said, "anything that could tell us more about the Seed home world, or the Seed themselves."

"But this place looks like it's been underwater for a million years," Karjan said.

"It probably has," Alan replied.

"Computers. Boards. Anything similar to what we have worked with before, but more complete specimens," Zu said as he climbed down to the floor. "I can take those to the labs."

"Found the door," Tier called.

The group turned around and followed Tier. The door was open, trapped inside its wall pocket. Outside the room, a long, dark hallway—a central corridor covered thickly in plants, sediment, and biologic growth.

"Well, aren't we lucky? This looks like an artery," Alan said as he shone his light up and down the hallway. Water dripped noisily from the ceiling and landed in pools.

"This looks like a cave," Mup said.

"A million years of cave," Karjan added.

"I'll take it," Alan said.

"So which way is best?" Tier asked as he looked up the hallway.

"The tallest portion of the blister we cut into was that way, so I say we go that direction," Alan said, pointing down the hallway toward Tier.

"We have survey drones. Might as well gather data," Zu added.

"Yes, of course," Karjan said as he slung down his backpack. He quickly removed four yellow boxes, placed them on a level shelf of matted sea plant, and activated each box with a touch. The boxes lit up and hovered a few inches off the ground, strobing a blue light.

"Survey the area, but don't go too far out. Message me if you find anything," Karjan commanded the fleet of drones.

"And record everything!" Zu interrupted.

"Record everything," Karjan added.

The drones exchanged flashing light codes and quietly took off in pairs in both directions of the hallways.

Karjan pulled out a small tablet and watched a map appear as the drones moved about.

"They're working."

"Let's go look around," Alan said.

"Split up?" Tier asked.

"We could cover more ground, but we might waste a lot of time if we get lost or need to work together to move something," Mup replied for Alan.

"I agree with Mup," Zu said.

"Yes, let's head together up that way," Alan finished.

The group turned and clambered up the hallway, following one set of drones that had already gotten thirty yards ahead.

The walk was hard, as it required climbing over piles of fossilized sea growth that blocked the hallway. Mats of plant life covering the ground often made movement treacherous with slips.

Karjan's tablet bleeped. Tier stopped and looked at Karjan.

"The drones ahead found something." Karjan read the tablet. "The hallway ahead opens up into a large chamber."

"Our lucky day!" Zu exclaimed.

The drones had indeed found a large chamber. The hallway fed directly into a wide entrance that opened up to a large room, two levels tall with a barely recognizable catwalk that lined the perimeter. In the center of the room, on the first level, was a single elliptical ring like the large outline of a conference table.

As the group's flashlights explored the room from the entrance, Alan realized the walls were textured with large hexagons a few feet in diameter; the surface resembling a lattice of filled honeycomb.

Alan turned his attention to the other features of the room. A domed ceiling explained the raised feature they had seen from the outside. A large staircase descended to the main floor.

"Without having seen much else, this seems significant," Alan said.

"How significant?" Tier asked.

"Significant to have that arterial walkway end, or start, here," Alan said. "And that ring down there. It could be their version of a bridge or command area."

The group shone their lights on the mysterious hollow ellipse marking the center of the room.

"I'm also interested in what these are in the wall," Alan said. "They cover the sides."

"Decoration?" Mup asked.

"No," Zu interrupted, "there is something about them that seems — purposeful. They have some utility. If not, I would be surprised."

"Let's look at that feature in the center," Alan said.

The group moved down a set of stairs and arrived in front of the elliptical feature.

"It looks like some kind of workstation," Zu added as he observed the shape of the feature.

"I agree," Alan said.

"It's kind of tall," Tier added.

"The Seed were kind of tall. Didn't you see how high the ceilings are and how awkward the stairs felt?" Alan replied.

"And the door controls," Zu added.

Alan looked to Zu. "Oh, I didn't even see those."

"That's how I recognize the controls on the workstation," Zu replied, looking over the surface of the terminal.

Alan studied the surface, wiping away stray bits of seagrass and a muddy layer of sediment. Underneath, a pattern of indentions revealed themselves. Alan fit his finger into the indention and imagined who had built it — who had touched it.

"Tier, Karjan — record all of this," Alan said, transfixed. "Record everything. This is going to be underwater soon."

Tier handed Karjan a small recorder, and Karjan began scanning the computer terminal and panning across the room.

Mup, on the opposite side of the workspace from the others, kneeled and inspected the base with his light. Panels.

Using his finger to clear away the edges of a panel, he uncovered a slide lock that had been hidden underneath a glob of mud. He pulled out a small metal pick and pried away growth from the lock, freeing it. Pulling the slide, the panel extended slightly, just enough to get fingers behind every edge. Mup continued pulling, and a block of metal the size of a small case came free. He flipped it over and got a view of the end that had been hidden. Electrical connectors in some form.

A computer.

Mup swung around his backpack, removed a bulky blanket, and in its place discreetly put the computer. He sealed up his bag and put it back on.

Suddenly, a shivering moan trembled through the vessel, and the floor shifted slightly.

"The wind," Alan said.

"Or worse," Zu added quietly, "the sea."

"Alan," Mup said as he rounded the computer terminal, "look at the base. These panels are computers of some kind. This is certainly some kind of important console."

"Given the central location, the shape of the workstation — this has to be a control room," Alan replied.

"If we clear away all this muck, we might be able to pry one of these computers out," Mup added.

"Maybe we could hot-wire one," Alan said thoughtfully.

Tier and Karjan turned. "You can do that?" Tier asked.

"If it's possible, he's our best bet," Zu said from afar as he walked the walls of the room. "He's the founding father of Seed computer research. But you better hurry. The storm is moving faster than we thought."

Alan pulled his pack off and dug through it. "Mup, clear one of the panels and see what you can get."

Tier and Karjan moved closer to observe.

"The Seed are certainly advanced, there's no disputing that," Alan said as he pulled out a beat-up metal case and balanced it on his pack, "but like nearly all civilizations, they use plain old electricity."

Alan opened the case to reveal a set of coiled red-and-black wires and a thick block with a small computer screen.

"And like Zu said," Alan continued, "I can't claim to be the galactic expert in much, but on this, I certainly hold the title."

Mup removed a block from the base of the workstation and illuminated the interior. Tier and Karjan knelt to watch.

Alan moved his bag closer to the empty panel and got on his knees to inspect with his light.

"Well, you were right, Mup. This is certainly a computer of some kind. Tier, Karjan, make sure you get this." Alan motioned with his flashlight. "In the back, you can see what looks like… communication ports. But, yes… there is a familiar sight. Electrical."

"So, what do we do?" Mup asked.

Alan looked at Mup. "Give it power. But if something goes wrong, don't tell anyone it was me."

"Couldn't that damage the ship? Isn't this an artifact?" Mup said.

"It's been under the ocean for millennia. I'll be surprised if it doesn't damage my tool," Alan replied as he began fitting probes to the electrical connectors.

"Okay, I can give power to this workstation for maybe a few seconds. Let's see what—" Alan clicked on his tool. The tool lit up, and from underneath the layers of sediment, the computer unit lit up as well.

Zu yelped from across the room. The group turned just in time to watch one of the blisters on the wall extend outward.

A column twice the length of a man had emerged out of the wall, briefly lit up, then flickered out into darkness.

Alan turned back to the workstation, which had also gone dark.

"I think that's all the play we get for today. Let's see what we unlocked," Alan said as he unhooked the device.

"Alan, come see this!" Zu shouted as he looked over the column with his light.

As Alan and the others walked over, the vessel shuddered, and a deep rumble rolled through the halls into the chamber. The group stopped and listened as the rumble continued and was replaced by the sound of rushing water. A flow of water from the far end of the room spilled over the catwalk and onto the floor, moving through the space toward the hallway. The waterfall quickly shrank into a wall of dripping water.

"That must have been a wave," Mup said, alarmed.

"We need to get going soon," Alan replied.

"Alan!" Zu snapped.

Alan turned to look at the object of Zu's alarm.

The column was a clouded shaft of plastic in which the silhouette of a tall, naked humanoid was visible. The creature's skin was dark on the outside and light in protected areas.

Zu moved his light up the body to the face. "A Seed," he said, shocked.

Alan looked at the face. A creature of untold age, lying frozen in a chemical suspension, waiting for this moment — to be rediscovered.

Alan looked at Zu, the two locking eyes.

"The wall features — they are long-sleeps, and this is — "

"A Seed colony ship," Zu finished.

"This will change the universe," Mup said softly.

From the center of the room came the sound of a crash and metal scattering over an uneven floor.

The group turned their lights to the sound and found Tier and Karjan standing by the workstation with a crumple of metal at their feet.

"What was that?" Zu asked.

"The beacon," Tier replied.

Stunned, Zu blurted, "How?"

Tier reached behind his back, produced a pistol, and fired bolts of plasma into Zu and the Seed tray.

As Mup pushed Alan away from the blasts, Zu fell back into the wall and collapsed. Mup rolled to the ground and drew a pistol, releasing a frenzied volley of shots back at Tier.

Chapter 16
Revealed

A wave of water rushed through the hull of the Seed vessel and poured into the pitch-black chamber where Tier stalked Mup and Alan. The water fell in a torrent over the edge of the catwalk and spread through the room, finding its way along wall edges out to a hallway on the lower floor. As quickly as it started, the water stopped flowing in.

"The tide is rising. Soon, this will all be underwater again," Tier taunted from the darkness. "But not before we vaporize this wreck. The sea cannot be the only vault for this secret."

Vaporize? A bomb? Alan wondered.

Alan crawled quietly in the darkness over the wet, muddy floor toward the far end of the center console. When the shooting had started, everyone flipped off their lights and scattered. Mup had disappeared into the shadows, and Alan worried that in the darkness, Mup's blasts might find Alan in error.

Tier unstrapped his backpack and felt Karjan take it away as it fell. Karjan walked quickly in the darkness until he touched one of the catwalk's supporting pillars. He felt the pillar's girth and positioned himself on the side he sensed most likely to be opposite of Mup's blasts. He lowered Tier's backpack and unsealed it, feeling inside and removing the bulky crate they had cared for so carefully since landing on the planet.

He laid the crate on the wet floor and felt for the latches, unlocking and opening it. A blue glow from inside the case spilled out, and Karjan used Tier's backpack to smother what he could. Inside the case were two metal cylinders and a small computer interface straddling between. Karjan at once began working the computer.

"You look at this vessel, and you see it for what it was and what it is," Tier continued. "You don't see it for what it will be — what it will do."

Tier let his words echo and die, the sound of dripping water filling the darkness. Somewhere in the room, a muffled crunch. Behind Tier, the sound of Karjan working discreetly.

"If you take what is here to an unready galaxy, you will kill a million stories of creation. You will kill a million gods — and with them the millions of civilizations that sprouted from those ancient beliefs. And what is gained?" Tier stepped slowly, listening for a stray footstep or a break in the water drops. "Billions suffer for your own egos. I can't let you continue."

Alan reached with his hands and felt the cold metal structure of the center console. He pulled himself to it quietly, safe for the moment. He shed his backpack and tucked it under the console but kept his switched-off flashlight in hand.

The shudder and rumble of a massive wave colliding into the ship repeated. The familiar sensation of seawater rushing into the chamber room returned.

This time, Alan found himself directly in the path of the icy ocean water. It poured over him like a sudden raging river. The water pushed, violently wrenching at him and trying to drag him away. He held on to the console desperately and waited for the wave to pass. The torrent weakened and subsided. Cold and wet, Alan controlled his gasp for breath — locking every muscle in his body as to not give himself away.

Tier listened as the sound of the water rushing around the room and down the hallway faded. Mup had a pistol, but did Alan as well?

"On Praxan, we had a beautiful world. Hierarchy and harmony. Every person knew their role and their place — every person was needed by the whole," Tier said. "Holding it together was *Pratana*. God, as you know it. For a thousand generations, our civilization knew peace and self-actualization — until the Core Alliance arrived and taught us better. Brought us out of the dark. It destroyed our culture — replaced our unifying myths with self-destructive *truths*."

Tier stopped walking. Mup and Alan were out there, listening.

"At the end of it all, when our youth were aimless, our families broken, and our communities' ghosts among packed cities of lonely creatures — the Core Alliance, the colonialists, didn't feel ashamed. They were proud to have brought us down to their level.

"I am sad that the Core Alliance won't see what we stopped them from doing. They won't see this vessel get scattered all over the ocean floor and know what truths will be lost forever. They won't know that a Praxan stopped them."

A loud squeal erupted from the case in front of Karjan and settled into a steady metronome of beeps. "The bomb is armed! Five minutes!" Karjan shouted.

Alan switched on his flashlight and lobbed it over the console toward Karjan's voice. It arced through the air and landed far behind Karjan, with a wet clatter, stopping against a wall and diffusing light weakly over the room.

Blasts from a pistol erupted near Alan and peppered the illuminated column Karjan was hiding behind.

As soon as the shots were out, Alan could hear Mup dash into the shadows under the catwalk, over the continued beeping of the bomb.

Tier didn't fire back. He won't give away his position unless he has a sure shot, Alan thought.

Alan got up and sprinted toward a wall, getting away from where Mup had fired his shots.

Tier watched in perfect silence from the shadows. Mup and Alan were both by the far end of the console. Mup had sprinted into the shadows on port, and Alan had made the mistake of dashing to the starboard wall instead of staying hidden behind the console. If Alan had a gun, he should have fired it by now. Mup was the threat. Alan was the distraction.

Karjan felt his right leg with his left arm. Two shots to his right side, and he couldn't move that arm or leg. *Lucky shots, damned lucky shots.* Everything in the vessel was so wet, he couldn't tell if he was soaked from blood or water. The bomb was still beeping loudly.

Tier walked slowly through the darkness. "You can't stop the bomb, and there is only one way out. You need to make peace with your God before I find you or the bomb kills us all."

Alan moved silently along the wall, edging closer to his destination—a body lying against the wall. Alan felt Zu in the darkness, trying to feel for his chest. Instead, he found Zu's arm and followed it to his hand. Zu's hand weakly squeezed Alan's, and Alan squeezed back. Alan moved closer to Zu.

"Show everyone," Zu whispered. "Show everyone what we found." Zu pushed a flashlight into Alan's hand.

"I'll be back for you," Alan whispered as he took the flashlight.

Another rumble formed, and the sound of the ocean finding a way into the vessel developed. Air rushed out of the hallway, turning from a howl to a sputtering jet of mist until, at last, a column of water shot from the hallway into the chamber. The room filled with chaos as seawater rushed noisily towards the end of the room.

Karjan heard the river of oncoming water and realized his weakness instantly. He couldn't escape the water, nor could he swim. The river of rushing water engulfed him and swept him away mercilessly, out of the chamber and down a dark secondary hall into the bowels of the ship. Karjan screamed in vain as the water pulled him under and he tumbled away in the roiling black maelstrom. Down the hall, the water swept, deep into the darkness of the vessel.

The water rushed away, and the torrent turned into a stream. The roar faded, and the only sound that remained was a small stream of seawater from the catwalk. The bomb was no longer heard. Dim reflections of light from Alan's flashlight cast the silhouettes of a stairway dramatically across the room.

"It is hopeless for you—the bomb can never be reached now," Tier said.

He's right! Alan realized. *There's no chance to get to the bomb now — it and Karjan are deep somewhere in the ship.*

Alan backtracked along the wall, staying in the shadows. He had to deal with Tier quickly to escape before the bomb detonated, but he didn't know where Mup was or what he planned to do.

There are two of us and one of him — but we can't use the advantage! Alan thought to himself.

Suddenly, Alan saw a silhouette cross between himself and the console, moving away from where Karjan had been. His mind raced.

I hope that's not Mup. Alan aimed the flashlight at the figure and turned it on.

Bathed in brilliant white light, Tier reflexively covered his eyes with an arm and released two plasma shots at Alan. From across the room, behind the console, Mup appeared and guided one blast into the back of Tier's head.

Tier's lifeless body crumpled to the floor in a muddy splash.

"Alan!" Mup shouted as he leapt over the console.

"I'm alive," Alan replied from the ground. "His shots went right over me." Alan rose from his prone position on the muddy floor. His front was covered in black sediment and stray sea debris from the floor.

"Nice teamwork," Mup said.

Alan turned the bright light to where Zu rested as Mup arrived. Zu lay on his side, his face in the mud and his chest and leg stained dark red with blood. "He's alive; let's get him out of here."

Mup ran over to Zu and squatted beside him. He listened for breathing and searched Zu's neck for a pulse.

"He's dead, Alan," Mup said.

Alan stared at Zu's limp body in disbelief. "He can't be! He was just alive!"

"I'm sorry, Alan," Mup said. "We have to go; we don't have any time."

"But he just said…"

Mup read the expression on Alan's face. "Alan, we have to go right now or Tier wins. What we have seen is still up here." Mup pointed to his head.

Alan realized Mup was right. "Okay. Up the stairs."

Mup switched on his light, and the two worked through the room to the stairs. As they climbed, Alan looked back at Zu. He couldn't help but feel he was abandoning him, and grief tightened his throat.

"Alan, we don't have much time," Mup called from the catwalk. Alan turned back up the stairs and ran to follow Mup.

The two could see sunlight filtering in from a room ahead in the hallway. They navigated over the lumps and piles of debris that had accumulated and made their way into the room with the hole in the ceiling. Water dripped from above.

"I hope those 'steeds are still there," Mup said, looking up at the water falling.

Alan climbed the pile of metal that had served as a landing pad for the climb down. The pile worked equally well as a ladder. Mup followed closely behind Alan, struggling to fit his body and backpack into the column they had cut.

Rising above the hull, Alan was greeted with a chilly rainstorm and a single wet Heliosteed stepping back in surprise.

"There's still one!" Alan shouted down.

"One will do," Mup replied.

"And the sea is back."

A stiff wind was blowing over the ship, pelting Alan's face with cold rainwater. The sea had risen to surround the vessel.

Where there had been naked ocean bed were now angry dark seas — waves breaking up and down the length of the ship in explosions of white.

Alan ran to the Heliosteed and coaxed the anxious creature into lying down so the riders could get on its back. Just as it obeyed, a wave broke nearby, and the winds carried seawater across the bird and men. The Heliosteed croaked loudly in a disapproving tone.

Alan climbed on and Mup quickly followed. Alan could feel Mup struggling with the saddle belt.

"Get your feet in the stirrups!" Alan shouted.

"I gotta get my belt —"

"Forget the belt — stirrups! Get your feet in the stirrups!"

Mup struggled to fit his feet properly.

"Forget it! Hold on tight!" Alan shouted.

"No, wait, I almost —"

Alan yanked the reins, and the bird leapt to its feet and thrust into the air with one stroke of its massive wings. Alan felt Mup's arms squeeze tightly around his chest.

The bird flew quickly toward land, sensing Alan's urgency. Alan guided the sprinting Heliosteed toward the rising forest and the central mountain.

Get behind the ridge!

The mountain and forests in front of them lit up in a sudden, brilliant white light and slowly began fading. Just as the bird crested over the first line of ridges a tremendous bang swept past and became rolling thunder.

The bird dived the backside of the ridge and skimmed the treetops. Mup turned to see if they had escaped danger, only to see an enormous white-and-black dome of steam rise from behind the ridge. Through the dome, streaming vapor and enormous chunks of the Seed ship arced through the air and over them. Pieces of ship and rock began falling from the sky and punching holes in the forest canopy.

Faster! Faster!

The Heliosteed was equally motivated to survive and kept a shallow dive while sprinting over the forest.

A tumbling, curved span of metal the size of a small building fell slowly from above in front of the riders. Without needing to be commanded, the Heliosteed banked to the right as the object crashed into the forest and kicked up a storm of debris. The bird curved back to the left and angled for the shoreline of the ocean ahead.

"Get us down!" Mup shouted.

"Working on it!"

Rock and metal fell like artillery, leaving explosions of dust where they landed. A gray shoreline appeared, and the Heliosteed arced parallel to the tree line and braked to a stop, landing on the sand of the beach.

Chapter 17
Resolution

Mup and Alan slid off the back of the bird and ran to the tree line of tall pines that bordered the beach. The two men reached the base of the trees and fell to the ground, sitting in the sand and rocks and pine needles. The Heliosteed hopped to follow, and the three watched from the false safety of the pine trees. White explosions of water peppered the ocean before them as the last remnants of the Seed ship fell from the sky.

As the group watched wordlessly, Alan, for the first time, noticed the storm moving over the island. The pine trees whistled and swayed as a steady current of air pushed through their branches and rain moved in sheets overhead. The skies were filled from horizon to horizon with dark-gray clouds, ripping and churning in torment. The ocean waters surrounding the island were capped with white waves, betraying the violent winds that followed the storm.

"I can't believe that just as I got to like the guy, as we finally came to truly understand each other — he's gone just like that," Alan said.

Mup watched the ocean quietly.

Alan spoke. "All the work he's done, all the labs he set up, the funding he arranged — all in the pursuit of making sense of each tiny clue we got about the Seed civilization."

"And then he died surrounded by thousands — hundreds of thousands of Seed themselves. Almost like a fairy tale," Mup offered.

"I guess that's true. When you say it like that — maybe he was lucky," Alan said.

"Maybe."

The two sat quietly, sheltered from the rain by the trees.

"He said something to me before he died," Alan offered. "He told me to show everyone what we found." Alan laughed to himself and continued, "Imagine that. I hated him for so long because all his work was hidden, but his last words to me were to make sure that I show everyone the greatest discovery of his life."

The breakers along the shore crashed with a subtle thunder.

"To come this far, to find that ship — to *know* what it was and to know its potential," Alan said, "and then to see it all destroyed in that moment. To see it all raining down from the sky. Nothing left."

Mup listened, staring out to the ocean. Then he sat up stiffly in a moment of realization.

Alan continued, "I think I could get used to living on an ocean island forever. I can't go back to Denarii empty-handed. Not after all that we've seen."

Mup reached for his backpack and unfastened the seal.

"There are Heliops somewhere on this island," Alan said, "Ocean Heliops. I'm sure they know how to fish better than I do. We can live with them."

Mup stared down into his pack.

"Mup, what is it?" Alan asked.

Mup looked at Alan. "We aren't empty-handed. In the ship, I grabbed this." Mup opened his backpack wide and revealed a Seed computer.

Alan laughed as he stared at the computer. He looked at Mup. "You sneaky... unbelievable! This is the second time you've come to me with a Seed artifact!"

"Remember what Zu told you?" Mup asked.

Alan smirked and nodded.

"You know what we have to do then," Mup said, looking at Alan and pointing a finger straight up.

Alan looked over his shoulder at the forest behind, the ocean in front, and then to the stormy sky above.

Mup continued, "No one is going to be looking for us on Ceto. They are going to come looking for us and are going to find our ships in a pit on Helios and assume we died. We have to go back."

Alan looked out at the ocean and sighed. He lifted himself out of the sand to go prepare the Heliosteed for flight.

"You know, Mup," Alan said, "we are a good team."

"I agree," Mup said as he sealed up the backpack.

Alan lowered the Heliosteed into a prone position and waited for Mup. The creature ruffled its feathers in anticipation, shaking off the rainwater that had settled. Mup, snapping his backpack on tightly, approached the bird and climbed onto its back, carefully getting into position in the second spot. He reached for the straps that formed the riding belt and carefully began putting them on. Alan climbed onto the creature and settled into the pilot position.

The two riders quietly checked their straps and footing once, twice, and a third time. Alan took the reins and summoned the bird into a standing position. It turned to face the ocean and looked into the storm swirling above.

"Alan," Mup said, "when we get back to Denarii, who should we say discovered the artifact?"

Alan paused for a moment, surprised by the question. He looked over his shoulder. "Zu."

Mup smiled and braced for flight.

With a whistle and a yank of the reins, Alan commanded the bird into the air. The Heliosteed and two riders lifted into the sky and made for the storm back to Helios.

Thank You

Thank you for reading Explorer's End!

If you enjoyed this book, please leave a review! You can find the links to this book on Amazon, GoodReads and others at hwportland.com/review

For behind-the-scenes notes from the author regarding the writing of this book, the process, inspiration, characters, and locations, please visit hwportland.com/eenotes

If you would like to contact the author directly, he can be reached at hw@hwportland.com

For updates on new releases and sales, join the mailing list at hwportland.com or follow @hwportland on social media.

About the Author

H.W. Portland has spent 20 years in technology working in the areas of healthcare, space exploration, and construction. He has traveled extensively around the world: he drank with strangers in North Korea, camped at a dump in Uzbekistan, and got lost in the Atlas Mountains of Morocco. He and his wife share their home on the Central Coast of California with two daughters and a large vegetable garden.

Visit H.W. on the web at hwportland.com.